1.

Gina was statuesque. That was always the first word that came to Felicia's mind when she looked at the other woman. Statuesque. A goddess. Amazonian. Those were other words people threw around when discussing Gina, and they discussed her a lot. Gina turned heads anytime she entered the room, and it was rare that she ever paid for her own drinks at bars. Felicia scanned Gina with her eyes as the other woman adjusted the strap on her bikini. There were times when Felicia wondered if Gina ever noticed her eyes on her, hungry, wanting, waiting. Sometimes Felicia was sure Gina could feel her eyes watching, but she knew that Gina was always aware of someone watching her.

Last week they were out a restaurant, Gina wore a skin tight, blue crop top. The top let Gina show off her impressive cleavage and stopped just above her navel, showing off the woman's solid, toned abs. She wore a matching blue skirt that clung to her every curve. At some point, Gina leaned over the bar to catch the bartender's attention. Felicia knew that once the young kid serving drinks caught sight of Gina's cleavage it would be all over for him, but Felicia noticed something herself. Gina was wearing a thong under the dress, and the raised lines of the inverted "T" of the undergarment pressed up against the thin fabric of the skirt when she bent over. Felicia couldn't take her eyes off of it. It was a moment, a brief moment, then Gina turned away from the bartender and saw her. Felicia quickly adverted her eyes, pretending to be looking at something at the other side of the restaurant.

"I don't know," Gina pursed her lips as she stared at her own reflection in the mirror, snapping Felicia back to the moment. "It just... doesn't work. What do you think?"

Felicia met Gina's eyes in the mirror.

"Oh, I, uh... I think it's fine."

Gina looked over her reflection again and shook her head.

"No, doesn't work."

She turned around to admire her ass in the mirror. Felicia pretended to be eying up the bikini critically. Gina could make granny panties look sexy. She was a tall woman, hence the "statuesque" and "amazon" comparisons, standing at six-foot -two with long brown hair that fell to her shoulder blades.

Gina stepped over to a clothing wrack and admired several other bikinis of various colors hanging from it. The one she was wearing was deep crimson, with blue rhinestones lining the straps and both cups, bringing a nice glittery accent to Gina's sizable bust. Felicia knew that Gina had breast implants, and always reminded anyone of that when they asked, but no one cared. The implants allowed Gina's breasts to stand large and firm, a nice solid D-Cup. They looked exquisite, the type of breasts that men spent long hours fantasizing about.

Gina wore a matching thong bikini bottom, also with rhinestones running along the hips and down the sides of the crotch. In the back of the bikini, instead of the typical "T" shaped back that most thongs have, was a series of red rhinestones that formed an upside down triangle. A small, crimson string ran down from the rhinestones and through Gina's sculpted ass cheeks. Felicia took pride that her ass was better than Gina's... at least that's what most told her. There was nothing wrong with Gina's backside, it was small and tight. The chiseled muscles of her butt clenched tightly whenever Gina moved. Her ass rounded out into a peach like shape at the bottom and then Gina's long legs started.

Much like the rest of her body, Gina's legs were a work of art. She spent the majority of her time in the gym, and it showed. Her entire body was lithe and sinewy, and Gina definitely didn't skip leg day. Also, much like the rest of Gina's body, her legs were a light shade of brown, a benefit of all the time Gina spent at the beach.

"I don't know, which one do you think?" Gina motioned to the bikini rack.

" Maybe the yellow one?" Felicia mentioned.

Gina pulled a small yellow bikini out, regarded it with her large, brown, quizzical eyes, and shook her head.

"This happens before every competition. I always have to pick the perfect one."

"What's wrong with the one you have on?" Felicia asked. It had taken Gina an hour to settle on this one.

"Too flashy. Not good for a competition." Was Gina's curt reply.

Felicia sighed. "Too flashy" meant too easy. As soon as Gina strutted out on stage wearing that bikini she would have all of the judges, all of whom were men, in the palm of her hand. The judges always adored Gina anyway, she won every competition.

All of Gina's bikinis, including the one she was wearing, were of her own design. Even the one Felicia was currently wearing was designed by Gina. Gina worked as a fashion designer when she wasn't modeling or training for another bikini competition.

"What are you wearing?" Gina asked absentmindedly as she went through the rack for the third time.

"Well, this." Felicia stepped back and swept her hands down her bikini clad body.

She wore an aqua blue bikini, with rhinestone accents similar to Gina's. The only difference was that hers was a typical "T" back thong bikini. Gina turned and looked her over, furrowing her brow.

"You're wearing that?" She shrugged and turned back to picking out a bikini.

"Yeah, what's wrong?" Felicia asked.

"Oh nothing." Gina didn't turn back to face her.

"No really, should I put something else on?"

"If you like it, then wear it." Gina shrugged again without turning back to face her.

Felicia clenched her fists. What was Gina's problem? This was her damn design anyway, Felicia didn't have to wear it. She considered what it would be if she beat Gina in this competition wearing another designer's swimsuit. Wouldn't that be something? Well, beating Gina in a bikini competition would be something indeed. No one beat Gina, she always placed first, and smiled through her teeth at Felicia and congratulated her when she came in second.

"Maybe I should see if I have something else to put on?" Felicia asked.

Gina only shrugged and picked out a black bikini.

"It wouldn't hurt to try a few different looks. We still have time." Her eyes danced over the bikini in her hand, but never once did she actually look at Felicia.

"You think?" Felicia asked.

"I'm sure that by the time you find an outfit, I'll still be looking."

"Okay, well I'll be in my dressing room. Let me know if you need anything."

"I will. Good luck if I don't see you before."

"Yeah, you too."

Felicia stepped towards the door. Gina turned towards the mirror and held the black bikini under her chin. She squinted and studied her own reflection like a surgeon would a patient. Gina's bikini collection ranged from any type you would see someone wearing at a beach to the more professional, competition kind. Tonight's competition was a straight up bikini pageant, so the competitors didn't have to get all tanned up and buff. All the girls had to do was go out and strut their stuff on stage in their best bikinis, and the winner got a five thousand dollar check and the chance to meet with agents and managers.

With a nod, Felicia stepped out of Gina's dressing room. The hotel hallway was surprisingly quiet, but Felicia knew that the closer they got to the competition, the crazier it would get. In the final moments before stage, the hallway would be a flurry of designers, trainers, managers, hair dressers, make up artists, and scantily clad women in various states of undress. Felicia looked up and down the hallway and then walked the few steps to her dressing room. She had no intention of changing, but needed an excuse to leave, but the look Gina gave her when she asked about her bikini was burned into her mind. Her bare feet padded on the soft carpet and she gripped the dressing room door, right next to Gina's.

Felicia let herself in and closed the door behind her. Inside, she found herself facing her reflection in a full length mirror. She took a few steps forward and ran her fingers under the straps of her bikini. She thought this color worked for her. Like Gina, her skin had a light tan, Felicia hated to get too dark. Her hair was also a light shade of brown, made all the more lighter by her blond highlights.

She turned to the side and examined her profile. Her boobs definitely were not Gina's, but whose wear? They were still impressive, and real, C-Cups. Felicia turned spin to look over her other side and admired the way her breasts jiggled and heaved when she moved. The bikini gave her cleavage an extra push as well. With another spin she had her back to the mirror, and she turned her head to peek over her shoulder. The thong made her ass look fantastic. It was nice, solid, round, and firm, and in her opinion, her best physical trait. When she was out, she liked to wear tights or yoga pants because of the way it accentuated her backside. Her legs straightened and the muscles in her butt clenched, putting a choke hold on the thin green fabric of the thong.

Gina's just jealous because this looks better on me than her. Yeah, That was it. She turned back around and nodded at her reflection to reaffirm this. Also like Gina, Felicia spent most of her free time in the gym. Her body with lithe and sinewy, and her abs were a solid six pack. Felicia flexed and admired the small peaks of her biceps and allowed herself a smile. It was at a gym that she met Gina, and they gradually went from gym buddies to a mentor/student relationship. Of course Gina saw herself as the teacher, spotting Felicia at the gym and offering training and diet advice. After six months of training, Gina asked Felicia if she had ever thought of competing professionally. At first Felicia declined, the stage wasn't for her.

Then her tuition bills came.

Felicia was in her final year of school for Criminal Justice at UCLA, and was planning on entering the police academy, but with the way her tuition bills were stacking up, it was looking less and less like she would even graduate. In the end, Gina convinced her, saying that she could use the money from competitions to pay for school, even score an agent and some modeling gigs. Right now, the money she was making was barely getting her through school, and the gigs were few and far between.

Then last month Gina came up to her, a big smile on her face. She had texted Felicia about hanging out and getting a drink, said she had news. It was the night Felicia saw the thong pressing through Gina's skirt.

Once they had their drinks, Gina revealed the big news was that she had been accepted to UCLA for Criminal Justice too. Felicia remembered hearing that and going numb. The restaurant, Gina, the world around all went quiet. Gina was outclassing her as a model, and now she wanted to do the same to her law enforcement career. There was no way she would let that happen.

Felicia came from a line of policemen, her father, his brother, their father and his three brothers, and so on. She was an only child, and her parents tried to discourage her from pursuing law enforcement, but she wanted to make Daddy proud. There was no way she would let Gina take this away from her, especially tonight.

Gina didn't need the prize money tonight, or the agents and managers. The real reason Gina was doing it was for fun, because she knew it would be an easy win. Felicia wouldn't allow it. She was dangerously close to getting get kicked out of UCLA, thanks to her back tuition and her grades slipping, and tonight could at least get her caught up with one of those. As for her grades, well if she spent less time competing, and more time studying, she could fix that.

She turned away from her reflection and over to a small closet on the side of the room. Felicia opened it and stepped inside leaving the door just slightly open behind her. The closet was small, but Felicia was able to fit in comfortably. Her jacket and street clothes were the only thing occupying the space for the moment. Set low in the wall was a small, ragged hole, and she knew exactly where it was because she had drilled it herself the previous night. Felicia told the organizers of the competition that she and Gina had to have private dressing rooms, and they had to be right next to each other. Seeing how Gina and Felicia were two of the biggest bikini competitors in town, the event was all too happy to oblige. The previous night she had shown up at the hotel and insisted that she had to inspect their rooms first hand or else neither would compete, sneaking a drill in with her gym bag.

She got on her knees and pressed her eye up against the peephole. It gave her a perfect view into Gina's room. Right now, Gina was still looking in the mirror, only this time she held a nude colored bikini up to her chest. And she thought the rhinestone bikini was too flashy? Yeah right. At the moment, Gina still had the crimson rhinestone bikini on. Gina turned around and admired her ass in the mirror, and after a moment hung the nude bikini back on the rack. Felicia knew that in a moment two burly, masked men would burst in the room, bind Gina's hands and feet, gag her, and carry her off. The competition would continue, but everyone would be talking about Gina. What happened? Did she walk out? Why didn't she compete? It would be the talk of the night, until Felicia won first place. She would of course thank Gina in her speech, citing her as a friend and inspiration, and she would solemnly state that she was sad that Gina wasn't there to compete that night. The next day, Felicia, concerned about the whereabouts of her friend, would burst into the dingy basement of a broken down tenement and find Gina at the mercy of her captors. Felicia would bring the two men to justice and save Gina. It was a beautiful picture, Gina, still gagged, her eyes wide and terrified, watching as Felicia strides forward confidently, ready to free her. For the rest of their lives, Gina would talk about how she owed everything to Felicia, and how bringing the kidnappers to justice had given Felicia a leg up on her fellow students in the police academy.

Felicia smiled at the thought and ran a hand along her right breast. Her and the men had never spoken face to face, all communication was purely by e-mail. She had specifically told them to gag Gina because she wanted to hear Gina's helpless, pathetic muffled cries as she got carried off. Gina deserved to be helpless, to be at someone else's mercy. Through the peephole, Gina turned so that her ass faced Felicia, and started to slide down her bikini bottoms. A gasp escaped Felicia's lips. The glittery collection of rhinestones slid down past Gina's tailbone and along her ass crack. Reflected in the mirror, Felicia could see the front of the bikini slowly sliding down along Gina's hips. Felicia's hand ran along her breast and she could feel her skin breaking out in goosebumps. A shiver ran through her body. Her nipples hardened and went erect. The bikini bottoms were almost halfway off. Felicia watched the mirror as more and more of Gina's smooth, shaved crotch was revealed.

Then she stopped, the rhinestone back clinging on halfway down her ass. Gina looked herself over in the mirror and turned to the side. Felicia's left hand slid along her thigh, stroking the skin gently. As far as she could tell, Gina was still clueless, but didn't push her bottoms down any further. The other woman continued to study her own reflection with a quizzical look. After a moment, Gina pulled the glittering thong back up. Meanwhile, Felicia's hand slid up her thigh towards her crotch. Through the peephole, Gina pushed up on her bra, watching as her own breasts heaved and fell back into position.

Felicia's hand slid under her bikini bottoms and she realized that she was wet. Any minute now, any minute they would burst in. She placed her other hand on the wall to steady herself. In her perceived privacy, Gina had started to undo her bikini top. A quiet moan escaped Felicia's lips as her hand slid down to her moist vagina. Soon-

-The door opened behind her and light spilled in. Felicia jumped and pulled her hand free-

-A rough, gloved hand clamped over her mouth.

"ULLUMMMMMMMMPH!" She cried into the stifling hand as she was dragged back out of the closet.

Her arms and legs flailed, her hands clutching at anything she could find. Another pair of gloved hands grabbed her kicking feet.

"UMMPH! MMMPH! ULLLMMMPH!" She cried, flailing helplessly in her captors arms.

They dragged her out into the dressing room and closed the closet behind them. Her hands swatted at the man who's hand was currently pressed tight over her lips. Her left hand clawed into his arm and found the thick fabric of a jacket. As for her right hand, it went high and found the softer fabric of a ski mask. She dug her nails in.

"GLLLLUMMPH!" She exclaimed.

"Uggh! Hurry up man!" The Captor yelled.

The other man, the one that had her feet, held tight and pulled a length of rope from his jacket pocket. He was dressed in all black and also wore a ski mask.

"UMMMMPH!" She tried to kick but he held her feet firm. In minutes, he had wrapped the rope around her ankles and knotted it.

"GLLLLMMMPH! MMMMUMMMPH!" She kicked her bound feet up and down, but the man had moved up towards her arms.

Her struggles became more desperate, and she groped around, trying to find the eyes of the man who held her.

"Fuck! Come on dude!" He screamed and pulled his head away from her flailing hands.

The other captor jerked her hand away from the other man's face and grabbed her other hand as well.

"MMMMMMPHH! UMMMMMMPH!" She tried to twist her head away, get her mouth free.

"Turn her over!" The second man ordered.

"I can't or she'll scream!"

"Then gag her!"

Felicia's eyes widened.

"MMMMPH! UMMMPH! MMMMPH!"

Her head shook furiously as the second captor pulled a white cloth from his pocket and wadded it. The man behind her took his hand away.

"Heelll-UMMMPH!" Her cry was cut off when the cloth was shoved into her mouth. She gagged, tasting the cloth as the captor lodged it deep into her mouth.

"Turn her over!" The second man ordered.

They spun her onto her stomach as she moaned into the cloth.

"Ummmmph! Hllllummph! Mmmph!"

Her arms were twisted behind her. She heaved and spit, feeling the cloth work free of her mouth. Yes! She spit again, working the cloth free with her tongue.

"Oh no!" One of the captors cried and forced the cloth back into her mouth.

"MMMMMPH!" she cried out in frustration.

After forcing the cloth in, her pulled out another white cloth and wrapped it around her mouth, forcing the stuffing into her mouth. The man pulled the cloth tight, jerking her head up, and then knotted it at the back of her head.

"Mmmmph! Ullllummmph! Glllrrrrpph!" She cried in frustration and shook her head, trying to work the gag loose.

Meanwhile, the men had crossed her hands behind her back and tied them just as quickly as they had tied her feet. She felt their hands come away from her. She shook her hands, bound tight.

"Mmmmph! Mmmmph! Ummmph!"

She wriggled around on the floor, moaning into her gag. Who were these men? What did they want?

"Okay, let's get her up." One said.

She tried to twist her body but felt one of them wrap his hands around her waist. In a moment, she was pulled to her feet.

"MMMMPH!" She moaned indignantly.

The man pulled her into a standing position, keeping one arm wrapped around her waist to keep her standing, while the other masked man stepped in front of her and studied her. The ski mask left only his eyes exposed, and he studied her for several minutes.

"Mmmm! Gllllmmmm!" She pleaded through the gag, widening her eyes as best she could.

The man gave her a curious look and then reached into his jacket pocket and took out a folded up piece of paper. He unfolded it, studied it, studied Felicia, and then studied the paper some more. After a few minutes, he held the paper up next to her face, his eyes darting between the two.

"Grrrmmmph!" She growled.

The man's eyes widened.

"Uh, I don't think we got the right chick"

"What?" Asked the other.

"It's the wrong one." said the one with the paper.

Felicia's eyes widened. These were the men she hired to kidnap Gina!

"Ummmph! Ummmph!" She nodded her head in agreement.

"Give me that!" Said the other one. He let go of Felicia and stepped forward.

Without the kidnapper to keep her balanced, she wobbled precariously, trying her best to stand on her bound feet. Both kidnappers peered at the paper, no doubt the photo of Gina she had sent them.

"Mmmm....mmmm....ummmm" she moaned into her gag.

Both masked men looked at the photo and then up to Felicia.

"What do you know! It is the wrong chick!" The other exclaimed.

"Mmmmmph! Mmmph!" Felicia nodded in agreement.

"Well, what do we do with this one then?" One asked.

"Lmmmph ummm mmmmoo!" Felicia mumbled into the cloth. If only they could take out the gag, then she could explain.

"What's that?" One of the goons asked.

"Lmmmph ummm mmmooo!" She turned her head in his direction and shook her head.

"I think she wants us to let her go."

"Mmmmph! Mmmph!" She nodded.

"Yeah, but then she's gonna squeal on us."

"Ummm Ummm!" She shook her head.

"Maybe we should just get the hell out of here!"

"Mmmph!" She shook her head again. Dammit she had already paid these guys half of their fee, promising the other half once she knew they had successfully captured Gina, but now they were gonna screw it all up. Then again they came pretty cheap, so she apparently got what she paid for.

"No, we have a job to do. Let's just throw her in the closet and get the other chick."

"MMMMMPH!" Her eyes widened. No! They couldn't do this!

"Good idea." The other man agreed.

"MMMMPH! MMMPH!" She protested as one wrapped his arms around her waist and started dragging her towards the open closet. Her bound feet kicked and flailed but to avail.

In moments, they had her in the closet and propped in the corner.

"Now you just stay here missy, we'll call later and tell someone about you. Sorry for the mix up."

"Mmmmph! Mmmmph! Ummmmph!" She pleaded into her gag.

"Sorry honey, we really are. Just try to be comfortable."

"GRRRRRMMMPH!" She screamed in rage, her eyes blazing with fire. Both men backed away and closed the door, plunging her into darkness.

"MMMMMPH! MMMMMPH! MMMMPH!" Felicia cried, but she knew it was no use.

She hopped forward, struggling to maintain her balance. There was no way she was letting these idiots get away like that. With another hop she found herself pressed against the closet door. Standing on her tip-toes, she started to spin around, taking great care not to fall over. Her bare ass cheeks brushed against the wood of the door and she relaxed against it, letting the door hold her up.

"Brrmmmph..." she sighed into the gag. It was a small victory.

Felicia slid sideways along the door until her bare ass cheek found the cold metal of the handle. Her bound hands reached out, gripped it, and gave it a turn.

It didn't budge.

"Ummmm..." She groaned and tried the handle again. No movement. Locked from the other side.

"Grrrrmmph! Ummmph!" She cried out in frustration and slammed her thonged ass into the door. The door didn't budge.

"Grrrrmph!" Pain shot through her back side and she rubbed her bound hands along her cheek as best she could.

"Ummmlllummmmph!" She whined and slid down into a sitting position. Now what?

Light, a small circular shaft of light shone through from the back of the closet. The peephole!

Still on her knees, Felicia shuffled forward. Maybe she could get Gina's attention.

Then what? Her plan would be effectively ruined, Gina wouldn't be kidnapped, and would win the competition. In fact, Gina would be her rescuer, something else for her to hold over Felicia's head.

She shook her head. It didn't matter, her plan was fucked anyway, and she sure wasn't planning on spending the competition bound and gagged in a closet.

Felicia pressed her eye against the peephole. Gina was still in her locker room, in fact she had changed. Now she was wearing a hot pink string bikini. The bottom was nothing but a thin string of pink fabric that ran through Gina's backside. The other woman stood with her hands on her hips, admiring herself in the mirror.

"MMMMMPH! UMMMPH!" Felicia cried into her gag. Here she was, bound, gagged, and helpless at Gina's mercy.

Gina stopped and turned her head.

"MMMMMPH! MMMMLLLUMMMPH!" Felicia cried out again.

Gina's eyes widened and she looked toward the direction of the peephole.

"Hello?" Gina asked.

"UMMMMMPH! MMMMMINNNAA! MMMPH!" Felicia called again.

Gina took a few steps forward.

"Felicia, is that you?" She asked.

"UMMMMMPH! UMMPH!" Felicia replied, nodding her head.

Through the peephole, Felicia saw Gina take a few more steps closer. Then Gina froze as a loud BANG echoed through her dressing room. It was the door being thrown open. Gina turned and her eyes widened. It was the kidnappers!

"MMMMPH! MMMMIIINNAA! MMMMPH!" Felicia cried out.

"Who are you!" Gina demanded and stood firm, hands on her hips like a superhero.

"This is the one." Felicia heard one of the men say.

"I'm giving you until the count of three to get out of my dressing room or so help-"

Both of the men descended on Gina. Felicia had a perfect view

through her peephole. One of them quickly ran behind her and

twisted both her arms behind her back.

"What are you doing! Let go of me right now!" Gina screamed and

kicked.

The other goon grabbed a pair of yellow bikini bottoms from a table

and shoved them into Gina's mouth.

"Get away from-UMMMMPH!" Gina's demand was cut off as her

mouth filled with her own bikini.

The same goon grabbed the matching bikini top from the table and

started to wrap it around Gina's mouth. She fought and kicked as the other one kept her arms behind her back, but soon her bikini top was wrapped around her mouth several times and knotted at the back of her head.

"GRRRRMMMPH! UMMMPH!" she cried into her gag, eyes blazing with fury. She shot out one of her long legs to kick at the kidnapper but he backed out of their reach.

The goon grabbed an aqua blue bikini from the rack and tossed the top to his accomplice.

"Here, tie her hands."

"MMMPH!" Gina tried to pull away but the man behind her had a firm grip. In moments, her used the bikini top to secure her hands behind her. He held her as the other man used the red bikini bottoms to tie her feet together. The whole time Gina's eyes blazed with fury.

"Grrrmmph!" She snarled at the man as she finished tying her feet together.

Felicia watched helplessly as the man behind Gina hooked his arms under her armpits.

"Okay, lets get her out of here."

"MMMMPH! UMMMPH!" Gina struggled in his grasp as the other man grabbed her feet.

Both of them lifted, one holding her by the feet, the other but the arms. Her hair whipped around violently and she screamed into gag, not out of fear, but rage.

"FFFFMMPPH! MMMLLLLLUMMPH! GRRRRMPH!

ULLLUMMMPH! GRRRMMMPH!"

Her head thrashed about as they carried her towards the door.

"Damn, she's feisty!"

"Shut up and let's get her out of here!"

"MMMMMMLLLUMMM! GLLLLLLUMMMPH!

URGGGLLUMMH!" Gina screamed into her gag.

And then they were gone, out of the peephole's field of vision, but

Felicia could still hear Gina's muffled cries.

41

"ULLLLUMMMPH! MMMMLLLUMP! GLLLLUMPH!
URRRGGLLMMMPH!"

Felicia heard the door to the dressing room close, cutting off Gina's
cries.

"Grrrrmmph!" Felicia exclaimed and knocked her head into the wall.

They had Gina, and here she was, alone and helpless.

TWO YEARS LATER...

2.

Deputy James Randy loved Marston's Pointe. He was a local boy,

born and raised, and the town was as much a part of him as he was

of it. Marston's Pointe wasn't a perfect town, but in the summer, it

was as close as anywhere could get, in his opinion. It was a beach

town, with a perfect view of the Pacific Ocean, and in the summer,

the ocean wasn't the only great thing to view. Summer time brought

in a whole mess of tourists, their money, and their swimsuits. Oh

boy, Randy smiled at the thoughts of the girls in their little bikinis, sunning, playing volleyball, swimming.... What more could you ask for?

The town lived for the summers, and so did he. During the day there was the beach, and at night, there was the Lady Luck Casino.

Randy always thought the girls at the beach were something, but when he went into the casino for the first time and saw the women, his heart nearly stopped. Apparently, after the girls were done at the beach, they put on their finest and hit up the casino, and not only that, but there were the waitresses and dancers there too. Word has it that Ace flew in the finest women to be a dancer at the Lady Luck, and paid them top dollar too. Every night men would turn out to watch the dancers there and fantasize about spending just one night with any of them, but those dreams never came true. After the women danced, they went on their merry old way, rumor had it that none of them lived in town. That's all anyone really had on Ace and any of his businesses, just rumor and hearsay.

On this particular morning, Randy was driving along Lookout Road, the main drag of Marston's Pointe, which ran along the beach. It was morning, and the sun hung high in the beautiful May sky. Randy always drove along this road, for... the sights. Sure the beach was nice, and the sky, but it was the joggers that really made this road special. He loved watching the girls run along this road in their tights or running shorts. In his opinion, it was the best part of waking up.

Like the girl he was currently watching. Randy drove at a normal pace, not wanting to seem like a creep, the last thing he needed was for some girl to catch an officer of the law rubber-necking, but this jogger caught his eye as soon as he turned onto the road. He didn't know her, which was rare, he knew almost everyone in Marston's Pointe. Chicks dig a dude with a badge and gun, at least that's what he told himself.

This particular jogger wore black tights that may have well been painted on. The tights stopped around her calves and accentuated her

46

perfect ass. Deputy Randy kept shifting his gaze between the girl's ass and the road, as to not get into an accident. He was on his way to meet the new sheriff, and didn't want to get into an accident on the way because he was gawking. But damn! The way each cheek lifted and clenched with her run, she was in shape alright. Her ass was tight and solid, he could definitely bounce a quarter off of it. Other than the tights, she wore a black sports bra, though he still trailed her so he didn't see what she was packing in the front. Her brown hair, with blond highlights, was tied back in a ponytail, and her skin was deep bronze. Ear buds trailed from her ears to what must have been an iPod clipped to the front of her pants, though he couldn't tell.

Randy wanted to pull over and start up a conversation, but what was an excuse for him to pull over? Maybe just to give a friendly hello? Cops could do that right? Of course he could, he was a deputy, hell he was the acting Sheriff!

Acting Sheriff. He still referred to himself as Deputy, and was happy as such. He never wanted the big office, but then Sheriff McFadden left town. Everyone saw it coming, but they still weren't prepared.

"That's what you get when you don't play along with Ace." Is what a lot of the people around town said, and Randy had to agree.

Ace could be your best friend or worst enemy, and McFadden refused to play ball, so Ace became the latter. That was six months ago, and Randy had been in charge ever since. It wasn't so bad, quiet mostly. Ace gave him a wide berth, and Randy extended him the same courtesy. Today was supposed to be the new Sheriff's first day, and Randy had taken it upon himself to be the welcoming committee, but the new Sheriff could wait a few minutes, couldn't he?

A car horn honked, bringing Randy back to reality. Another vehicle was behind him, and riding very close. Whoever it was had stones, honking at a cop car, but he suspected they knew why he was driving so slow.

The jogger slowed and turned her head. Shit!

Randy hit the gas and sped up. *Nice going James Randy, you just looked like a total creep!*

As he pulled ahead, he allowed himself a quick glimpse of the jogger in his rearview. She had stopped, and her breasts were almost as great as her ass. A sheen of sweat hung over her cleavage, and her breasts heaved up and down as she caught her breath. The sports bra held them in place perfectly. An iPod was clipped to the very front of her black tights, pulling them down slightly, exposing a hard "V" cut just under her abs, almost two arrows leading right to her-

Randy blinked and turned back to the road. He couldn't get distracted now, but holy shit, this chick! He would have to drive along at this time more often, maybe get a name or something. He turned his attention back to rear view to see that she had started jogging again, though was growing steadily smaller in the distance as he drove on.

3.

Fifteen minutes later, Deputy Randy turned off of Lookout Road

onto Overlook Avenue. It was a residential Street, but it was one of

the most sought after places to live in Marston's Pointe due to the

view it had of the ocean and easy access to the beach. Randy

whistled, how could the new Sheriff afford digs like this? Homes

lined both sides of the street, perfect little suburban homes with

perfect yards and perfect paint jobs, and the expensive cars in the driveway. His GPS announced that he was at his destination: 2932 Overlook Avenue.

Randy pulled over and killed the engine, surveying the Sheriff's house. It was a quant two story house, with attached garage and a fence surrounding the front yard, probably the back too. A car sat in the driveway, telling him that someone must be home. He took a breath, trying to collect his thoughts, it was the first day and he wanted to make a good impression. The Deputy took another look at the quiet street, there was something familiar about this place, but what was it?

Oh no! Randy took a breath and smiled, realizing that he knew this part of Overlook very well indeed. The Sheriff lived right next door to Tanya Donnelly. Donnelly wrote for the local paper, *The Marston Observer*, and also fancied herself as something of a armchair detective. She was very active in the neighborhood watch, and a regular at the police station, constantly badgering them with her latest theories or clues about crime in Marston's Pointe. Most of the cops ignored her, and as far as Randy knew, she wasn't on Ace's radar... yet. Tanya was a piece of work though, and living right next to the Sheriff meant that the Sheriff would never get a break from her. His gaze shifted to another house, this one across the street. The bushes and hedges were trimmed perfectly, the lawn cut to a uniform size. It was Shelly Arnold's house. Shelly too was a piece of work, but for much different reasons.

Once again, Randy shook his head, pitying the Sheriff, who was about to get a rude awakening to the world of Marston's Pointe. He gripped the door handle and was about to exit the vehicle when a familiar sight jogged around the bend. It was the girl, the jogger from earlier, and she was heading his way. He leaned back and watched in the rearview, she looked even better up close. Her whole body was slick with sweat, and the iPod still tugged at the front of her tights, showing off her abs and that V cut. She slowed as she approached, unclipping the iPod to stop her music. The tights retracted around her slim waist, hugging her like a second skin. Finally, she came to a stop outside the Sheriff's house.

Holy shit! Was this the Sheriff's girl? Randy rubbed his eyes and blinked. She opened the front gate and approached the front door. This Sheriff was a lucky bastard to be banging a chick like this. He felt almost bad for ogling his new boss's girlfriend (wife?) like that, but he was allowed to look, right? Once again, he gripped the door handle, maybe he could get some chit-chat in with her, nothing wrong that.

He stepped out of the car as she was unlocking the front door. The sound of him closing the cruiser door caused her to take notice of him. Randy raised a hand in a wave.

"Hi there!" He said, smiling.

Hi there? Jeez, couldn't he come up with something a little more snappy?

The girl stepped away from the door and put her hands on her hips.

"Hello," she said, eyes inquisitive.

"I just... was in the neighborhood, thought I would stop by and welcome you to our small town." He kept smiling as he approached the front gate.

"Thank you, that's very nice of you." She said, still watching.

"I'm Deputy James Randy, well, until today I was Acting Sheriff. You can call me Randy." He stopped just outside the gate.

The girl stepped off the porch and approached him.

"Pleased to meet you, you can come in." She nodded to the gate and Randy let himself in.

"I must say, this is a wonderful home you guys have here, and such a great spot."

"Thank you, right now it's kind of a mess, unpacking and all," She approached and held out her hand. "Felicia, Felicia Fetters."

Randy took Felicia's hand and shook it. He tried to keep his eyes on her face and not her heaving, sweaty breasts. Damn, she had a great rack. The sun caught the sweat on her cleavage just right, giving her breasts a glow.

"Since it's our first day working together, I thought I would extend a welcome to you guys, maybe give an escort to the station."

"Us guys?" Felicia asked, her eyes narrowing.

"Yeah, you and the Sheriff." Randy said, admiring his ability to stay focused on her face.

"I think you're confused," she said. "I am the Sheriff."

4.

The Deputy's jaw almost fell clean off when Felicia told him she was the Sheriff. Immediately, he started apologizing profusely and rambling about how he thought she was the Sheriff's girlfriend or wife, though there was nothing wrong with women in law enforcement, and on and on, stuttering and stammering as he went. She put up a hand to invite him for a drink and to spare herself any more rambling. She lead him into the kitchen, which was about the only room fully unpacked so far.

"Water, Deputy?" She asked.

"Oh, sure, water's fine." He nodded and looked around the kitchen. "I just want to apologize again ma'am. I meant no disrespect. I just..."

"It's fine, things happen." She sighed and opened the fridge. The bottom of the fridge was lined with water bottles, and she bent over to grab two.

"I think a female Sheriff will be good for a small town like this, a good change of pace you know, a way to..."

He trailed off and Felicia turned around to see his eyes dart over to the kitchen window. She didn't have to be a mind reader to know he was checking out her ass. Hell, she could tell that he was barely avoiding staring at her chest earlier. Felicia grabbed two bottles from the shelf and closed the fridge.

She studied the man, the Deputy. He looked to be in his early thirties, with a small beer belly starting to form. He had his brown hair slicked back, but his widow's peak showed that it was already starting to recede. He had bright, eager eyes that had a very naïve quality to them.

"Heads up." she said and tossed him one of the bottles. Randy jumped and held out both hands, barely catching the bottle. He fumbled as it tried to fall free from his delicate grasp but finally he caught a firm hold of it.

Felicia sighed.

"I graduated UCLA with a degree in Criminal Justice, did two years with the LAPD, then decided the city life wasn't for me." She said and took a long swig of water.

Randy's eyes ran over her body while she drank. Her eyes narrowed and he jumped and twisted the cap off his bottle and took a quick drink.

"Well," he said, lowering the bottle from his lips. "We're glad to have you."

"I'm glad to be here. I hear the last Sheriff left suddenly."

"He had... family problems, decided to take up a less stressful position."

"Do things get stressful around here?" She asked and took another drink. Some water dribble out of the bottle, down her chin, and along her chest. She watched Randy's eyes as they followed the stream of water as it slid between her breasts.

"Deputy?"

"Oh, well, like any small town, people do get rowdy from time to time."

Felicia sighed. It seemed like there was something he wasn't telling her. She wiped her mouth and moved her hand down to wipe the water off her breast but thought better of it, instead choosing to rest her hand on the island in the center of the kitchen.

"One more question: where's a good gym around here?" She asked.

"Oh, um, Jerry's Kung-Fu has a gym in the basement." he said.

"No L.A. Fitness or anything like that?" She asked.

Randy shook his head.

"That will be all for now Deputy, I'd like to get a shower and then head to the station." She set her bottle down on the island and stepped away.

"Oh, sure." He said, still gawking at her.

"I'll see you there." She said, her eyes darting towards the door.

"Oh, yeah right!" He jumped and moved out of the kitchen. Thankfully he didn't turn around to see her shaking her head.

5.

Felicia showered quickly, did her hair and make-up, and wearing only a towel, stepped into her bedroom. Most of the room was boxes, with the exception of her king size bed and a full length mirror on the wall. She shed her towel and slipped into on a small, white thong and matching sports bra. From her suit case she grabbed a pair of police slacks and held them up to her waist. She hated them, they were baggy, sagging in all the wrong places, and had cargo pockets lining the sides. They were part of the uniform when she was in the LAPD, and she hated every minute she had to wear them.

She studied her reflection, why wear them now? She was the Sheriff, couldn't she dictate the dress code? Of course she could, and part of the reason why she took this job was because it was in a small town, things were more relaxed. Vandalism, maybe drunk and disorderly were probably the most extreme things she would have to deal with, so to hell with regulation pants. Felicia tossed the pants aside and studied her reflection. If only that Deputy could see her now, with her small thong disappearing between her toned ass cheeks, he would probably have a heart attack. Like the rest of her body, her ass was extremely tan. Back in LA, she would go to salons and tan nude so to avoid tan lines. With the beach right behind her, she figured she could tan there, but she wouldn't be caught sunbathing in the nude. Eventually she would have to find a tanning salon in town.

She turned around to study her ass in the mirror. Maybe tights would do. Yes, tights. They would still give her free range of motion, but she wouldn't feel like she was ready to storm the beaches of Normandy. With her back to the mirror, she grabbed a pair of tights and stepped into them, watching as she slid them up her legs, past her knees, her thighs...

The tights stopped just below her cheeks. She winked at her reflection and slide them up, watching as the black fabric eclipsed her rear and the white thong. After that, she threw on a black tank top and grabbed her tan, button up uniform shirt. The shirt fit well, but was meant to be tucked in.

I wonder if I can order a different kind of shirt? Maybe Sheriff tees or something?

She buttoned up the shirt and tied the front tails together. Once again she studied herself in the mirror. The knot at the bottom of the shirt hovered just above her tights, but something was off... Aha! Felicia undid the top few buttons of her shirt, exposing a little bit of cleavage. No one ever said that she couldn't enforce the law and look good at the same time. To tie it all together, she slipped into a pair of police issue boots, and then added her gun belt, complete with her Glock, taser, pocket knife, handcuffs, and a few extra clips. Felicia doubted that she would ever need her gun, or even the taser, but she felt safe with them. Then there was the handcuffs, which she certainly hoped she would never have to use. If she was a kinkier girl, she could maybe find recreational use for the cuffs, but she had told herself that she would never allow herself to be bound, not after that night at the competition, not after Gina...

Felicia shook her head, that was all behind her now. She had a new life here in Marston's Pointe, and was going to make a new name for herself. Lastly, Felicia reached over to a dresser and grabbed a gold, star shaped badge, her Sheriff's badge. It was the ultimate symbol of her authority in this town. She raised the badge up and pinned it onto her shirt, just above her left breast. The light from the outside reflected off the gold of the badge. Sheriff Felicia Fetters, now it was official. Finally dressed, she looked herself over in the full length mirror. It was time to kick some ass.

6.

Sheriff Fetters stepped onto her back deck and took in a breath of the nice, beach air. The house had a fair sized deck outside, and a small yard, but the yard didn't really matter. Her yard was fenced in, though a gate to the back lead to the beach, her real yard. She already foresaw plenty of tanning and swimming there in her future.

"Hey Ian, bring me out some lotion!" A female voice cried out from her right.

Felicia turned towards the voice coming from her next door neighbors. It was a house somewhat bigger than hers, with a deck, full patio, and in-ground pool, though Felicia didn't understand the point of a pool when you lived a few yards away from the ocean. Next door, a woman was laying on her stomach on a beach chair, and right now was giving Felicia an excellent view of her ass cheeks. It was an impressive ass, not big, but... full. The woman's cheeks were sizable enough that Felicia couldn't determine if she was wearing a thong or just nude. Her skin was pale too, and Felicia

70

couldn't help but think that this was the kind of person who didn't tan but just burned.

"Ian! My lotion!" the woman raised her head, showing off a mane of flowing red hair.

Felicia shook her head and stepped off the deck to the walkway leading to the front. Next door, the woman heard Felicia's boots on the wood of the deck and turned to face her. The woman's eyes went wide and she jumped up from her chair.

"Oh my God! It's you!"

Oh no. Either this woman recognized Felicia from her modeling days, or just wanted a word with the Sheriff, either way Felicia wanted no part of it. She hadn't even set foot in the police station yet, so she sure as well didn't consider herself on duty yet.

The woman stood and ran across the patio towards her. Felicia could now see that the woman wore a small, white, thong bikini. Like her ass, the woman had extremely large breasts, and they heaved and bounced as she ran over. She was curvy, and not the modern "curvy" which is just another word for fat, but curvy in the old fashioned, Marilyn Monroe way. It was obvious that the woman didn't work out, but her tummy was still flat and it seemed that all her weight went to her boobs and ass.

"You're the new Sheriff!" The woman yelled excitedly.

Felicia smiled and stepped over to the fence separating their properties.

"Yes, Felicia Fetters, nice to meet you!" She held out her hand.

"Tanya Donnelly." The woman smiled and held out her hand.

She was older, maybe in her forties or so, but she wore her age well. They shook and withdrew hands.

"Quite a grip you have there." Tanya said.

"So I'm told." Felicia still smiled.

"So a woman Sheriff huh, that's new." Tanya's eyes ran over Felicia, who had been in enough bikini competitions to know when an opponent is sizing you up.

"Yes, it's amazing how the world works" Felicia stepped back.

"Now if you'll excuse me, I'm due to stop by the station." Felicia started walking up the walkway and Tanya kept pace.

"You know, I would love to have a sit down with you. There is so much wrong with this town. Marston's Pointe has a major crime problem." Tanya explained.

"Does it now?" Felicia asked.

"Oh yes, I grew up here, and would love for my son to grow up in a safe, small town like I did, but drugs, prostitution, gambling, it's ruining it all!" Tanya's breast heaved as she ran along the fence.

They came to the front yard, Felicia hoped that being on the street would cause the woman's modesty to kick in and she would retreat back to the patio, but no such luck.

"It's that Ace, he's running it into the ground! I have gathered so much evidence on his activities, its unbelievable. That last Sheriff listened, and look what happened to him!"

Felicia stopped and eyed Tanya. They both stood in their front yards now.

"What happened to the last Sheriff?" Felicia asked.

"Ace ran him out of town, he was getting too close." Tanya's eyes were wide, she crossed her arms over her chest.

"Who's Ace?"

"Ace is in charge of it all, nothing goes on in this town without him knowing. It's his way or the highway."

"What more do you have on him?" Felicia asked.

"Just... Ace. Not many have seen him, or know where to find him."

Felicia sighed and stepped away from the fence. She didn't have time for this woman's conspiracy theories.

"Tell you what, why don't you come down to the station, bring what you have, and we'll talk." She said and headed for her front gate.

"Wait!" Tanya cried and ran for her front gate. Felicia caught a glimpse of Tanya's thonged ass jiggling as she hurried and unlatched her gate.

They met again on the side walk as Felicia took a step towards her driveway.

"Why don't you come over tonight! We can compare notes, have some wine."

"Look, I really have to go. Stop by the station, preferably with more clothes on."

Tanya looked down, as if it had just dawned on her that she was clad in a bikini, then back up at Felicia.

"Look, don't trust anyone, especially-" She pointed at a house across the street and Felicia followed her finger.

"Shelly Arnold, backstabbing bitch."

"Does she work for Ace?" Felicia asked.

"She works for herself, but will play along with Ace when she needs to. Plus, I always catch her son peeking out of his window at me while I'm by the pool."

Tanya stepped back, placed a hand on her hip, and stuck out her ass.

"I know that I'm a piece of work, but I don't like that pre-pubescent shit beating off to me."

Felicia nodded. This woman was a piece of work.

"Look, stop by the office, we'll discuss while I'm on duty. Have a good day" She turned away and walked towards the driveway.

"Thank you Sheriff! And be careful!" Tanya waved as Felicia walked away, and her bikini seemed like it could barely contain her bouncing bosom.

Felicia nodded. This was turning into quite the first day.

7.

"I'm telling you, you gotta see this Sheriff!" Randy exclaimed, eyes wide, hands waving in the air. Deputy Frank Olsen sat at the desk across from Randy and rolled his eyes.

"I'm not falling for this one James." He turned to face his computer, staring at nothing in particular.

"I'm serious man, she's like...wow!" Randy turned to his computer to bring up a search engine.

"Last thing I need is for Marcia to come in here with my lunch and see that I'm working for a woman that, in your words, is "a perfect

81

piece of ass".'" Frank reached into his desk and pulled out a package of zebra cakes that he kept stashed there.

Frank was a much older man, and extremely overweight. His wife, Marcia, kept him on a tight leash, and was always harping on him about his weight and heart. Everyone in the station knew that if Marcia found out about Frank's hidden stash of goodies in his desk, then she would string him up by the balls.

"Here man, let me show you." Randy turned back to his computer and typed in Felicia Fetters into a search engine. He took a sip of coffee while he waited for the page to load.

"Besides, what would a girl like that want with a town like this?"

"Chicks love the beach, man."

"Hmmph" the sound came from the other side of the room.

James turned towards the noise to see Deputy Alice Cringe sitting at her usual spot, the desk right in front of the main door. Alice was ancient, with short gray hair and coke bottle glasses. The woman had been on the force for as long as Randy could remember, and had been hunched over that desk since he started. She never went out on calls or investigations and mostly served as a receptionist because... well that was all she could do. She also had a radio set up at her desk along with a phone so that she could serve as their dispatcher. Most on the force thought that Alice should have retired long ago, but she was a stubborn old bat, and being dispatcher made her feel like she was a part of the team.

The three of them sat in the main bullpen of the station, a long room filled with desks arranged in three neat rows, though Frank and

Randy's were the only ones being used. At the back of the bullpen jutting out from the back wall was the Sheriff's office, which sat dark and empty. A doorway in the right corner of the bullpen lead to a long hallway that lead to the currently empty holding cells. Most of the time the cells were used a place where drunks could sleep it off for a night or so, Randy couldn't remember the last time they actually used them for a perp.

"Don't believe me either?" he poked at the older woman.

Alice turned, her bug eyes glaring at him through her glasses.

"I hope you're wrong because you boys won't get nothing done with a thing like that prancing around the station."

Randy grinned, took another sip of his coffee, and turned back to his computer.

What he saw nearly made him spit up his drink.

He gagged and quickly swallowed the hot beverage, it burned going down.

"Frank! Frank!" He croaked, catching his breath.

"What? What? Are you okay?" Frank jumped up from his desk.

Randy nodded, gasping, his eyes wide.

"Dude... come over and check this out." He exclaimed.

Frank stepped away from his desk and carried his girth over to Randy's desk., shoving a zebra cake in his mouth as he came.

"Might wanna swallow first." Randy warned.

Frank stood behind Randy's chair and bent over. When he saw the computer screen his eyes widened and he gagged on his treat.

"Come on, stay with me man." Randy patted him on the back.

Frank swallowed and looked at the screen. The screen was filled with a photo of a brown haired girl in the middle of an empty gym, her back to the camera as she faced a full length mirror running along a wall. It was a professional photo judging by the lighting. Her face intense and focused. She had a barbell in each hand, the veins in her arms bulging. Her hair had blond highlights, and wore a white shirt, the front ripped down the center, exposing her cleavage. Randy couldn't even call what she wore shorts, since they stopped halfway along her ass, exposing her full, hardened cheeks to the viewers. To top it off, her whole body glistened with sweat. It was Felicia Fetters, the Sheriff.

Both Randy and Frank gawked.

"This is the Sheriff?"

Randy nodded, closed the photo and opened up another one, this one of Felicia on a beach in a orange bikini that showed off her ripped physique.

"How... what" Frank stuttered.

Randy minimized the photo and brought up another one of Felicia posing on a stage in a green, glittery bikini.

"Says here she was a LA based bikini and fitness model." Randy said as he scanned the bio below the pic.

"So... she stopped to become a cop? How does that make sense?"

"I did it to pay for college." A female voice answered.

Both men jumped and looked up. Felicia stood by Alice's desk, her eyes narrowed at them. Frank let out a choke and stepped away from

Randy's desk. Randy hit the "X" at the top of the page, closing the window.

"Oh, Sheriff, we... um... just doing some... background..." He stuttered, standing up.

Felicia stepped away from Alice's desk towards them. She had the top few buttons of her shirt open, and once again Randy had to struggle not to gawk at her cleavage. Instead of the standard issue uniform pants, she wore black tights.

Both men stood straight, eyes wide as she approached.

"I've already met Deputy Randy," she said, zeroing in on Frank, "and you are?"

Frank wiped a hand on his shirt and extended a hand.

"Frank, Frank Olsen. Deputy Frank Olsen, ma'am." He stammered.

"You got a little..." She motioned to the corner of her lip and Frank brought a shaky hand up to his mouth, feeling the crumbs that collected at the corner of his mouth.

Felicia stepped away and looked past them to the empty office at the rear of the station.

"Is that mine?"

Both nodded.

She stepped past them towards the office when Alice's gravelly voice disturbed the already tense office.

"Excuse me young lady, what exactly is that you are wearing?" She stared daggers into Felicia.

Felicia spun around to face her.

"I'm relaxing the uniform requirements, see that as my first official act as Sheriff."

"But you're wearing that? Are we a police force or a dance squad."

"I have made my rule, if you don't want to dress like I do then that's your choice."

"I'm sure all the boys around here would love it if I came in wearing tights and my shirt open for everyone to-"

"Once again, Deputy, if you want to dress like this that is your choice and I will-"

"It's unbecoming of the Sheriff to-"

"If you don't like it then feel free to turn in your badge!" Felicia's eyes turned to fire, her fists balled.

Alice sat at the edge of her seat, her mouth agape. Somehow, her eyes seemed even bigger.

"Is that all, Deputy?" Felicia asked, gritting her teeth.

"Y-Yes Sheriff." Alice said as her eyes narrowed. She too clenched her fists.

"Very well then. And if anyone else has a problem with it, they too are welcome to leave."

Both Frank and Randy shook their heads.

"Good." Felicia nodded and turned to her office.

In a few strides, she was across the room and opened the door. She switched on the light. It was spacious and open, completely windowed so that whoever sat inside could see out into the whole station. Some file cabinets were pressed flat against one wall while a desk was pushed back against the far wall. Randy followed Felicia in as she surveyed her new office.

"No one's been in here since the last Sheriff left." He said.

"Well, first thing's first," She said and approached the desk on the far fall, "Give me a hand with this." She bent over and gripped the front of the desk.

Randy stifled a gasp. The fabric of her tights was thin, almost sheer. When she bent over, the fabric was stretched to it's limit over that ass of hers. He could see that the skin of either cheek was as tan as the rest of her, and that she wore a tiny, white thong.

"Well," She turned her head and he quickly met her gaze, "grab the other side."

"Oh, uh sure..." he said and shuffled over to the far end of the desk.

Randy shuffled to the far side of the desk, giving a straight on view of Felicia. She bent over, gripped her end of the desk, and pulled as Randy pushed. As he pushed, he looked up to see that she was looking over her shoulder as she pulled, but still bent over, and her cleavage hung over the desk like two plump cherries. His knuckles whitened as he gripped the desk, watching as her breasts rippled with each movement.

"Okay, stop." she said, letting go of the desk and standing straight. Randy too let go and stood opposite her.

"What next?" He asked. If he got watch her move stuff around all day, then that wasn't such a bad day at all.

She met his gaze and he could tell that there was something on her mind by the way she chewed her lip.

"This Ace character that I keep hearing so much about, what do you know about him?" She asked, placing her hands on her hips.

He stiffened. Oh Christ, Tanya must have gotten ahold of her!

"Look, just let it be. If you treat Ace good, he'll treat you good, you know?"

"That's not what I asked you, I asked what you know about him."

"Sheriff, he's not to be messed with. He owns most of this town." Randy was pleading. He didn't want to lose another Sheriff because they got in over their heads.

"And does he own most of the crime too?" Her brown eyes bore into him like lasers.

"No, well... according to rumor... nothing has been proven, you know?" he stammered, her eyes never leaving him.

"Okay, why don't you sit down and tell me everything-"

"Sheriff!" Alice's voice called from the other room. Felicia rolled her eyes and turned towards the older woman.

"Yes?" she asked.

"Got a call!" Alice shouted.

Felicia turned back to Randy.

"We'll finish this later." she said and headed out of the office. Randy followed.

He had to find a way to get her off of this Ace thing. He had heard stories of what happened to the people that crossed Ace, getting run out of town was getting off light for the last Sheriff, but Randy knew that Ace preferred to work with the police. Killing a cop, or a missing cop, meant attention that Ace didn't want.

Felicia approached Alice's desk.

"What is it, Deputy... I'm sorry, I don't think I ever got your name."

Felicia said with a note of apology in her voice.

Alice grimaced.

"You didn't," she folded her arms, "It's Cringe, Alice Cringe."

Felicia nodded.

"So what's the call?" She asked.

"Rossi's Bar and Grill, a vandalism call."

Randy went white. Oh no! This was about to blow up.

"I'll handle it!" he said and jumped forward.

"No," Felicia held up a hand, "I think it's time the people of this town got to know their new Sheriff. I'll head down"

"It's probably kids, you know? Nothing too big."

"Then it will be a good way to ease myself into things." She said and turned towards the door.

Randy chased after her and grabbed her arm. She spun around to face him, eyes flaring.

" I mean, it's just... you have so much to do here, I don't want you to get overwhelmed." His eyes were wide, pleading.

Felicia glared at him.

"I said I'll handle it," she shook her arm free of him. "Plus, I need to get to know this town. If it is kids, like you say, then it will be an easy call."

"I'll go with you." He volunteered.

"No, stay here in case something else gets called in."

"But Sheriff-"

"That's an order." Her face hardened. Randy shrank back and nodded.

"Yes ma'am." he said.

"Good," she looked over the station and her three deputies, "call me on the radio if you need anything, and thank you all for the... warm welcome."

She nodded and turned towards the door, all three Deputies watched as she exited through the glass doors. Randy had a bad feeling about this. There had been rumors that Ace was interested in acquiring Rossi's, by any means necessary. If the new Sheriff got mixed up in this, then... he didn't want to imagine.

8.

Felicia was driving for about ten minutes before she realized that she didn't know where she was headed and had to call back into dispatch for the address. She could practically feel that old battle axe... Alice was it? Whatever that woman's name was, Felicia could practically feel her bug eyes narrowing in disapproval as she spouted off the address. Dealing with this woman was going to be one of the first things Felicia would do as Sheriff, how old was she? Old enough to retire, she imagined. Maybe Felicia could offer her some kind of pension and get rid of her.

Her next order would be to hire more help. The station had room, plenty of it, but only two desks seemed occupied, three if you counted that old woman. What happened to all the other police? Felicia had counted at least six empty desks, and that was only in one room of the station. Then there was this Ace character, Randy seemed like he knew a lot, and probably did. There was also the way Randy reacted when Felicia said she would take this call, like he was spooked or something. She was convinced that he was hiding something from her and made a mental note to have a sit down with him later, that is if she could keep his eyes off of her cleavage.

She sighed as her GPS announced for her to make a left turn. Frank and Randy, she would have to do something about them too. As policemen, she had no idea how they were, but she constantly felt their eyes on her, not to mention that she walked in on them ogling photos from her modeling days. Maybe letting go of one of them would make it clear that she was their boss and not eye candy, but she quickly discarded that thought. First, she would have to find more help, then deal with those two.

Her mind kept coming to the photo they were salivating over, one of her in a gym. She was hoping that moving to a town like this would put her modeling days far behind her, but like her time in the LAPD, it seemed to keep haunting her. Officially, her explanation for taking this job was that she wanted to get away from the hustle and bustle of the city, but that was hardly the truth.

Felicia tightened her grip on the steering wheel, thinking back to that night at the competition, the night that changed everything. The last night she saw Gina. Of course, everyone involved with the bikini competition noted Gina and her absences, but she still spent the night bound and gagged in that closet. The next morning, a maid came in and heard her bustling about and let her out of the closet. Police and paramedics were called of course, but Felicia was in perfectly good health, just sore from being tied and gagged all night. There were questions, of course, and she chose to play ignorant. She told them that two men burst into her room, tied her, stashed her, and then left. It basically was the truth. But what about Gina? She had agonized over what to say about Gina, whether she should say that the men took Gina too, or just come clean with it all and admit everything. In the end, the police investigating guessed that the men that jumped Felicia probably took Gina as well.

And that was it, the last she heard of it. The cops all told her how brave she was, how tough she was, they promised to find her friend and the men that took her. But months passed and nothing. Felicia graduated and got a job with the LAPD, and had many long, sleepless nights where she wondered what happened to those men and Gina. There were many times that she thought about contacting them at the e-mail they provided, but she knew that would mean having to face the truth, and herself, and couldn't bring herself to do that.

She turned her police cruiser onto what looked like the main street of Marston's Pointe. Shops and restaurants lined both sides of the street, and people of all ages milled up and down the sidewalks. This was probably the place where all the tourists went when they weren't on the beach. It was cute, all of the shops seemed quant, and she spotted several cute looking boutiques. Maybe she would make a day of exploring around here soon, when she wasn't in uniform. The GPS announced that her destination was five hundred feet ahead. It felt good to be behind the wheel of a cruiser, especially one that was her own. As a side bonus, the radio barely went off, a sharp contrast to her days on the LAPD when it was constantly squawking and chirping. As she drove, she watched as a few heads turned to watch her cruise by, no doubt townsfolk realizing that she was a new face.

In a moment, she saw her destination. It was a small, two story building on a corner, *ROSSI'S* was emblazoned above the front entrance in big, red letters. Several neon signs advertising various beer brands hung in the large, front windows. As she pulled her cruiser to the curb, Felicia saw immediately why the police were called. The front door of the bar was at one time all glass with a wooden border, was completely shattered. Jagged pieces of glass jutted out from the wooden border like teeth, but most of the glass lay in glittering shards on the sidewalk and inside. Outside the bar, Felicia could see a woman with a broom sweeping up the shattered glass.

Felicia pulled her cruiser to the curb and killed the engine. Well, here it is, her first official call as sheriff, and it was most likely a simple vandalism case. She reached into her breast pocket and pulled out a pair of black shades, Aviators, and allowed herself a smirk. May was well look the part right? Looking in her rearview mirror, she slid on the shades and admired her reflection. Now she looked like a proper police woman, strong, authoritative, no nonsense. In the mirror, she could see the woman outside the bar starring at her. The woman had set her broom against the building and was waiting, hands on her hips. A gasp escaped Felicia's lips and she was thankful for the shades, which hid her widening eyes. This woman, most likely a bartender or waitress, was breathtaking.

The woman wore a small, grey hoodie with the zipper halfway down, exposing her full, deep cleavage. Her breasts, as well as the rest of her body, were a dark tan. Felicia could also see a hot pink strap of a bikini top running under the hoodie and along the woman's shoulders to a knot tied at the back of her neck. The bartender, or

waitress, had her auburn hair tied back in a ponytail and her brown

eyes bore into Felicia from under a pair of small, black framed

glasses. To complete her outfit, she wore small, cut off shorts. Hot

pink strings that were tied into wiry knots stuck out of the shorts on

either hip, suggesting that she wore bikini bottoms under them.

Despite wearing her shades, Felicia couldn't shake the feeling that

this woman knew she was being eyed up. Quickly, Felicia turned her

eyes away from the rearview and exited the vehicle.

As Felicia got out, she could see the woman cross her arms against

her chest, pushing her large breast up and in. The way they heaved

under the hoodie suggested to Felicia that they were natural.

"Are you from the Sheriff's office?" The woman asked with a raised

eyebrow.

"Sheriff Felicia Fetters, how can I be of service?" Felicia said, striding forward and extending her hand.

The woman's hands remained crossed. Felicia couldn't take her eyes off of her magnificent cleavage and was once again thankful for the shades.

"You're the Sheriff?" The woman asked, eyebrow still raised.

"Yes I am, first day on duty." Felicia smiled and crossed her arms.

"Janet Rossi". The woman said, and grabbed her broom. "So, is this how the police force will be dressing from now on." Her eyes scanned over Felicia's body.

Felicia's eyebrows raised.

"This is your business?" She asked. She had assumed that this woman was an employee, not the owner.

"Yes it is, for the moment at least."

Felicia took a step towards the shattered door. "Was anything stolen?"

"No," said Janet. "Just the door."

Felicia squatted down and examined the glass shards on the ground.

"Kids maybe? Angry customer?" she asked.

"I can see your thong."

Felicia's eyes widened.

"What?" she asked.

"Your little white thong," Janet said. "It shows through your tights."
She stepped past Felicia and into the bar.

Felicia stood up and crossed her hands behind her back and followed
Janet inside.

"Look, um... Mrs. Rossi?"

"Ms. Rossi." The woman rolled her eyes and turned to face Felicia.

"Ms. Rossi, I'll get a statement from you. Do you have security cameras or anything like that outside, maybe we can-"

"Don't bother, I already know who's responsible."

"Could I have a name?" Felicia said. This woman and her attitude were starting to wear on her, and she wanted this over quickly.

"Why, not like you'll be able to do anything." Janet turned away and stepped behind the bar. Felicia followed for a bit, but stopped on the other side of the bar.

"Try me." Felicia said. If this woman didn't want help, then fine, but Felicia would at least give it a try.

Janet sighed and turned towards Felicia.

"Look, I don't know why I even called you guys, I just... thought it was what I was supposed to do."

"Tell me what you know and I'll see what I can do."

Janet turned away again and bent over, reaching for a cabinet on the far wall. Felicia could see that Janet wore her cut offs with no belt, and they slid down, exposing a hot pink thong bikini underneath. There were several shelves in the cabinet, and whatever Janet was after clearly wasn't on the top one, so she squatted down to search

115

the second shelf. Her shorts slid down lower, and Felicia could see the pink of the thong disappear between the curve of Janet's beautiful butt cheeks. Like the rest of her, Janet's backside was well tanned.

"I can see your thong." Felicia said with a smile, unable to resist.

Janet wheeled around and glared at her, pulling a dust pan out from the cabinet. She stood up and jerked up her shorts.

"This was supposed to be my day off, I was going to spend it on the beach. Ace saw fit to ruin those plans."

Felicia's eyes widened again. Ace! She was getting tired of hearing that name.

"Ace? He's responsible?"

Janet sighed and stepped out from behind the bar.

"Ace runs most of the businesses here in town, I'm the most successful of his competitors. He sent his people last week to make an offer to buy me out."

Janet headed for the shattered front door and Felicia followed.

"Let me guess, you said no."

Janet turned towards her, there was a fierceness in her eyes, but also... something else. Sadness?

"My father spent every cent he had on this place, it was his life, his dream. I promised him that I would keep it going for him." She motioned towards the decimated door, "This is just the beginning, Ace will keep going until I give in."

Janet stepped outside and Felicia followed.

"What can you tell me about Ace? Where can I find him?" She asked.

"No one knows where to find him, he sent his goon, Jack, to talk to me."

"Where can I find him?"

Janet gave Felicia a quizzical look.

"You gonna stop him? The last Sheriff tried too."

"I haven't even been on duty one day and I've heard too much about this Ace. He's number one on my priority list."

Janet looked over Felicia with something that looked like pity.

"Many have tried, but he owns this town. You either play ball or you get thrown out of the game."

"I promise you, I will stop these people. You shouldn't be bullied into giving up your business."

Janet looked over the bar and back at Felicia, her hard exterior had somewhat diminished, and Felicia saw a strong but scared woman, a woman backed into a corner. There was something about Janet, something weary, but also a fierceness in her. Felicia tried to place Janet's age, maybe mid-thirties, but with a body that would make most 22 year olds jealous. But Janet's brown eyes though, they were weathered with experience, the eyes of a much older woman.

"Well good luck," Janet said, her eyes softening, "but I hope you know what you're getting into."

Felicia reached into her pocket and pulled out her note pad and pen and began jotting something down.

"I don't have business cards yet, but this is my personal number. Next time any of them make contact with you, call me."

She tore out the page and handed it to Janet, who once again gave her a quizzical look.

"Did you just give me your number?" She was smart, Felicia will give her that.

"For professional purposes only." Felicia reassured her, though she was kidding herself as well.

She looked Janet over again, wondering what she looked like with that hoodie off and those shorts around her ankles, but then shook the thoughts away. Right now, she was on duty, and had to operate as such.

"Well, if anything happens, I'll let you know." Janet stuck the paper in her shorts pocket. Felicia nodded.

"Please do." Felicia nodded and turned back towards her cruiser.

She was just about to get in when she heard Janet call after her.

"Hey!"

Felicia stopped and turned towards her.

"Just... be careful. These guys can be tough." She said, her hands wrapped tightly around the handle of her broom.

Felicia nodded and stepped inside her cruiser. As she drove away, her eyes kept straying to her rearview to watch as Janet worked at cleaning up the glass shards. Her beach day huh? She made a mental note to visit the beaches around here more so that she could see what

Janet looked like in her hot pink thong bikini.

9.

Felicia pulled into her driveway, killed the engine, leaned her head against the seat, and let out a deep sigh. Her first day as sheriff was officially in the books, and it had been a day.

Well, I wanted the big job, and this is what I get. She thought.

Ace, that name came up too many times today. A man who thought he owned the town, a man who thought he was untouchable. He was a man that everyone knew, but could never find. And then there was Jack, apparently one of Ace's lieutenants. She made this her first priority, somehow she would bring these men to justice. Everyone in the town seemed scared of Ace, so her first order of business would be to find people who weren't afraid of reprisals from Ace's men.

Her thoughts turned to Janet Rossi, the enigmatic bar owner. As much as Felicia tried, she couldn't shake that woman from her thoughts, her intense stare, her pink bikini...

Felicia shook her head. Now was not the time to be distracted. She already was struggling to get her staff to take her seriously, and she could only imagine what they would do if she started making advances on an attractive bartender with a rocking body. Right now though, she was home, and it was time to decompress. As she exited her car, she couldn't help but notice that the sky had gone to a deep crimson, and decided that the best way to decompress would be to enjoy the sunset from her back yard with a beer in hand.

After going inside, she went straight to the refrigerator, grabbed a beer, and headed for her back deck. The sun looked beautiful over the lapping waves of the ocean, and she shut the back door behind her and settled into a chair on her back deck. The ocean was a slightly lighter shade of red than the rest of the sky. She realized that she could get used to coming home to this every day after work. Maybe after she finished her drink she would throw on a bikini and go for a night swim.

I can see your thong. Janet's words echoed in her head, causing Felicia to frown. She didn't realize that these leggings were that sheer. Her frown deepened when she realized that everyone at the station could also see her thong.

Felicia tightened her grip on the beer bottle and took a deep swig.

Never again, she wasn't going to provide those clowns with more

eye candy than she already did. She took another sip of her beer and

stared out over the ocean. It was just her first day, things were bound

to be strange, she just had to adjust, make some changes...

She was snapped back to attention by the sound of a door closing.

She followed the sound to next door, seeing Tanya stepping out of

her back door. Felicia froze, not wanting to be cornered by her yet

again. But Tanya didn't even look in her direction, or even seem

aware of her. Tanya was dressed in all black, black jeans, boots, and

a black leather jacket with what looked like black tank top

underneath. The red haired woman reached into her pocket, pulled

out a small digital camera, looked it over for a minute, and then set it

back in her pocket. There was something about her manner that set

Felicia on edge.

Tanya scanned around the area, almost frozen, but somehow missed Felicia in the low light. Felicia sat frozen, watching. Once Tanya was satisfied that she was alone, she started creeping towards her back fence, slowly, on tip-toes. Where was she sneaking off to? Her head was constantly scanning the area around her, looking for... enemies? Who knows what went on in her paranoid mind. Still on tip-toes, Tanya reached her back gate and lifted the latch between two fingers. The metal latch let out a slight squeal of protest, causing her to freeze. Felicia leaned forward and narrowed her eyes.

Latch still between her fingers, Tanya stood like a statue. After a moment, Felicia saw her shoulders relax and she gently pushed the gate open onto the beach. Tanya gave a final look back at her house, and then slipped onto the beach, closing the gate behind her. It took Tanya an agonizingly long time to lower the latch, letting it lower inch by inch until she was satisfied that it wouldn't make any sound, and then she let it secure the gate in place. With the gate closed and latched, Tanya took off down the beach.

Felicia set down her beer by her feet. Where was Tanya sneaking off

to? She had a son, right? Maybe she was sneaking off to meet a

lover? But what about the camera, a camera she checked to make

sure she had. And there was the fact that Tanya was in all black, and

clearly on edge. Wherever she was off to, she didn't want people to

know, or to stop her. Tanya was a reporter, and seemed to have it out

for Ace and his goons.

Oh no.

Felicia shook her head, no, Tanya wasn't sneaking off to trouble,

probably just... just what? What else would she be doing? No,

Felicia knew that wherever Tanya was off to, it was nothing good.

I'm off duty. She told herself, call it in to the station, let someone else

handle it. But what if Tanya got hurt, or worse? If anything happened to her, everyone in the station would know that Felicia could have done something and chose not to. Felicia shook her head. Dammit! She knew it had to be her.

She was still in her uniform, hell, still had her gun belt on and everything. It was time to be sheriff. Felicia shook her head again and stood up. Tanya's trail should be easy enough to follow on the beach. Felicia gritted her teeth and took off towards her back gate. This was getting to be too long of a day.

10.

The sun hung low, casting a yellow light over the ocean while giving the rest of the night a blue tinge. Tanya's footprints were easy to follow in the sand, but Felicia cursed the steadily fading light. She was tempted to use the light from her cell phone to make sure she was still on the trail, but didn't want to risk the light exposing her. The lapping of the waves on the beach disguised the sound of Felicia's footsteps, at least she hoped. In the low light, it was almost impossible to tell how far ahead Tanya was, but Felicia took her time, not wanting to follow too close.

Exposing what? She thought, it's not like she had anything to hide. But Tanya clearly did, and Felicia didn't want to risk scaring the woman. Unless this was all for nothing and Tanya really was just sneaking off for a rendezvous with a lover or something. One thing was for sure, either Tanya was confident that she wouldn't be followed, or she knew nothing about covering her tracks. Or both. Felicia squinted in the blue glow of the early evening, once again picking out Tanya's boot prints on the beach, and continued onward.

The air was growing cooler as the light waned, and a cool breeze

blew in off the ocean. As the cool air hit Felicia, the thin fabric of

her tights did little to warm her, and she felt her bare ass cheeks chill

and break out in goosebumps. *Damn!* She had to find better pants,

tights were clearly a bad idea, though she still refused to wear those

bulky, standard issue uniform pants. A shopping trip was definitely

in order soon.

Another gust of wind and another chill, Felicia's cheeks clenched.

She felt like she may as well be pants less out here. A few yards

ahead, Felicia could see lights piercing the ever growing darkness.

She froze instinctively, waiting. Watching the beach ahead, she

could make a shadow making it's way towards the lights: Tanya. The

red haired woman was crouched low to the sand as she crept her way

along the beach. Felicia placed her hand on her holster and followed,

ready to draw her weapon if things went south.

As she moved closer towards the lights, she could see that the beach was running along what looked to be an industrial district. Street lamps illuminated several ominous, dark warehouses set along the water.

So Tanya most likely isn't having a romantic rendezvous, Felicia thought, her hand drifting towards her weapon. Large docks loomed out over the beach, and Felicia watched as Tanya climbed a set of service stairs leading up the warehouse district. After waiting a moment, the Sheriff followed, hand still on the butt of her pistol. The service stairs were old, rusted, eaten away by the salty sea air, and Felicia set a foot on the bottom stair. It was shaky but held. She took them one stair at a time, not wanting to make noise and alarm Tanya, or anyone else that may be around.

After what seemed like an eternity, she emerged onto a quiet walkway over looking the beach. *Shit!* She no longer had Tanya's foot prints to follow! Felicia stayed low and pressed flat against the wall of a warehouse, making her way along the walkway. Hopefully Tanya didn't go far. For a time, Felicia started to think that this area was deserted, the only sound being the lapping waves against the docks.

Then she heard voices in the darkness. Felicia froze. Damn! She pressed against a warehouse, hand ready to pull her weapon. It was hard to discern the voices over the waves, but they sounded male. After a moment, Felicia pressed on. The wall she was pressed against ended and she peeked around the corner, looking at a dark, paved roadway. Directly across the road from her was another warehouse, and beyond that, bright lights, and beyond the lights, the voices.

Felicia looked around but didn't see any sign of movement, then sprinted across the road and pressed against the side of the warehouse. The voices were louder now. Still pressed against the wall, Felicia peeked around the corner. A low pier hovered just over the water with a boat tied off to it. Men were unloading boxes from a boat and carrying them to a small warehouse located just off the pier. There was no sign of Tanya. After a moment, Felicia ducked back along the wall. There was no way she could approach from this angle, the men would see her, and Tanya hopefully thought the same. Who were the men? They couldn't be dockworkers, could they? From her brief look, they seemed to be clad in all black and looked very rough.

Shit, this is bad. Seeing how Tanya was a reporter, Felicia could only guess that she was following a story, but these guys didn't seem like the type to give a reporter a good quote for a story. Felicia moved along the wall towards the street, hoping to approach the warehouse from the other side and get a good look at the men and what they were doing, and who they were. She reached the end of the wall and found herself in an open loading and shipping area. Crates and boxes of various sizes were stacked in neat piles all around, and also provided amble cover.

Felicia scurried out and and hid beneath a pile of small crates, giving her a view of the warehouse. Two large bay doors were open, letting light spill out, voices echoed from the inside. She scanned the area, searching-

-Yes, there she was. Tanya was crouched behind some wooden boxes a few yards away, in a position that gave her a perfect view inside the warehouse. She was also way too close, if anyone in the warehouse happened to look outside, they could see her watching. From her vantage point, Felicia could see Tanya reaching inside her jacket for the camera.

Dammit! Felicia stayed low and ran out from behind the crates. Tanya's back was to her, her attention focused on the men inside. In seconds, Felicia was on top of Tanya and clamped one of her hands over the woman's mouth while using the other to pull Tanya back.

"UMMMMMPH! MMMMMPH!" Tanya struggled and Felicia could the woman's lips smacking against her hand as she tried to call out.

"Shhh! Shhh!" Felicia said in her ear.

"MMMMMMPH! GLLLUMMPH MMMMM LLLMOOO!" Tanya struggled and kicked and Felicia dragged her into the shadows behind a large stack of crates.

"Shhh! Be quiet!" Felicia whispered.

"GLLLLLMMMMPH!" Tanya protested, her hands flying up and locking around Felicia's wrists, trying to pull it away. But Felicia's grip was too strong, and she pressed flat against the crates and raised her other hand, wrapping it around Tanya's chest and pulling the woman close.

"Shhh! It's Felicia, Sheriff Fetters!" she whispered. Tanya went still, but Felicia didn't move her hand.

"I'm going to take my hand off your mouth, but you have to stay quiet, okay?"

"Ummph!" Tanya protested.

"Okay?" Felicia asked, her tone icy.

"Ummmph!" Tanya nodded. Felicia moved her hand and crouched down, Tanya followed suit.

"What are you doing here?" Tanya demanded.

"I'm the Sheriff, I should be asking you the same thing!" Felicia wasn't in the mood for a pissing contest with this woman.

"I got a tip that Ace's men were bringing in a weapon shipment, I'm going to get photos and write the story tonight!"

"Are you crazy, they could kill you!" Felicia glared at Tanya, but the woman just glared back, her eyes blazing.

"Someone has to do something about these men!" She said, her face almost turning as red as her hair.

"Yes, and that someone is me. Now get out of here."

"I'm not leaving-" Tanya started before Felicia cut her off.

"No, you are. Get far from here, call my office, have them send men down. Tell them I'll be waiting."

Tanya's face softened with confusion and... concern? She stared at Felicia for a moment.

"What about... What will you be-"

"I'll be fine, tell my men to meet me here right away, and to come armed. We have to make a bust."

Tanya looked over Felicia, sizing her up.

"Will you be... okay?" She was concerned, and maybe proud. Felicia guessed that Tanya expected resistance.

"I'll be fine, its time these goons learned this town doesn't belong to them."

Tanya nodded and scooted away.

"Go!" Felicia ordered. Tanya nodded again and scurried off into the night. Once she was out of sight, Felicia let out a breath. That was one problem solved, now what about these men? She had to keep them in place until back up arrived, but how? She would have to make this up as she went.

She peeked out from behind the crates and was given a perfect view into the warehouse. A panel truck sat inside by a loading bay, several wooden crates stacked next to it. The weapons. Felicia didn't see any guards, everyone must be out on the dock unloading. Maybe if she could get in there, she could disable the truck somehow, that should hold them up until back up arrived. A few feet in front of her were two wooden crates stacked side by side, she took a look to see if the coast was cleared, and then dived out from cover towards the crates.

Felicia was bent low to the ground and scurried along the ground, dived down behind one of the crates, and landed in a crouching position. Her blood turned to ice when she heard a loud ripping sound.

She froze, pressed flat against the crate, listening. What was-

-She shivered as another breeze rolled in off the ocean, once again feeling the cold air on her bare ass-

-Oh no! Felicia's eyes widened and she ran a hand along her backside. She expected to feel the fabric of the tights but instead found her hand running along the smooth skin of her butt cheek. The thin fabric of the tights had split along the seam. Moving her hand further, she ran a finger around the exposed thong running through her buns. Fuck! Of all the times! She gritted her teeth and shook her head. This had already been quite the first day, but now she had to do a weapons bust with her butt out for the world to see. There was nothing she could do, it wasn't like she carried a spare pair of pants along with her just in case. Dammit!

Felicia spun around and looked out over the crates. Shit! Several men had moved into the warehouse from the back and were making their way towards the truck. She froze, preparing to duck down but the men made no indication that they saw here. It must have been too dark out here. This could work out somehow. Now she only needed a plan. In the warehouse, one man opened the back of the truck while the other looked over the wooden crates, no doubt filled with

guns. They were about to load up!

She shook her head, she needed a plan, or needed back up to get here

ASAP.

11.

Stand guard! Travis shook his head at the thought as he patrolled the

empty docks. Stand guard! Anyone could stand guard, hell, they could go hire some kid off the streets to stand guard. Travis had been with the organization almost six months now, starting off doing security at Ace's Casino. He was a bigger dude, having played football in high school, would have had scholarship too if he hadn't taken that bad hit and broke his leg.

After a month at the casino, Travis's boss asked him if he was interested in earning extra money.

"Fuck yes!" Travis said. He wanted out of this town. He was born in Marston's Pointe, raised in Marston's Pointe, and wanted to see something in the world that wasn't Marston's Pointe. His plan was to save up and get out, maybe L.A, maybe the East Coast? He would figure it out when he got there.

Mostly he worked as an enforcer, being brought along to shake someone down that owed Ace money, or track down a girl that tried to run off. He started by doing one job a week, but now worked almost every night. He hadn't me the big man yet, but from what he knew, not many did. Ace kept himself hidden well, and everyone knew that Jack was his mouthpiece. So of course, when they asked him if he wanted to be muscle for Jack on a weapons deal, he jumped at it. Hell yes, working with the second in command? This was his ticket!

Travis knew Ace had operations all along the west coast, and hoped that if he impressed tonight, then maybe they would send him out of town. At this point, he would take any detail that would get him out of Marston's Pointe...well unless they asked him to work with those hillbilly dudes that made the drugs for Ace. Everyone knew about those guys, the ones that stayed in the mountains just outside the town. No one went there alone.

But all of Travis's dream came to a halt when Jack told him to patrol around the warehouse in case there was a problem. Travis wanted to protest, but this was Jack, no one said no to Jack. So Travis

swallowed his pride and walked the lonely, empty streets of the

warehouse district. He was fairly confident that no one would dare

fuck with them, but if someone did... well there was just so many

places for someone to hide, how was he, one man, supposed to

watch them all? Part of him knew that Jack probably had other

guards patrolling, but still. How was he supposed to impress the boss

when he was on babysitting duty?

Travis almost thought he was hallucinating when he stepped out

from behind one of the empty warehouse. He circled the perimeter,

had a smoke, and circled back, figuring he should stay close to the

warehouse. As he came in sight of the warehouse he froze. There

was a woman crouched behind a small wooden crate, and she was

staring directly into the open bay doors of the warehouse. Travis

should be panicking but he wasn't, instead his jaw dropped and he

felt a stirring in his pants. The woman wore the brown uniform of

the Marston's Pointe Sheriff Department, and looked very attractive, especially from behind. Her ass was excellent, this he knew because the back of her pants had split open, exposing her round, tanned ass.

His eighteen year old brain tried to wrap itself around the situation.

She's a cop! Get it together dude!

But he couldn't take his eyes off her exposed rear end. Was she wearing panties? He couldn't tell, but it looked like she-

-No, there. The woman leaned forward and Travis could see the thin white fabric of a thong running between those magnificent cheeks of hers. Holy shit! Where did she come from, who was she!

She's a cop, and if Jack finds out you let us get busted because you were too busy ogling her, then you're dead!

Travis shook his head. Fuck, he had to deal with this! But fuck, a cop! How-

-This was it, his moment. He was being a look out and caught someone, a cop. Jack would be happy, especially since Travis got over the obvious distraction of her exposed ass. Travis didn't know who this lady cop was, but he owed her. Maybe once they had her on ice, he would kiss that amazing ass of hers.

He stepped forward and pulled his gun from his pants. The cop didn't turn or seem to notice. Good, keep focused on the warehouse.

It gave him more time to admire her ass anyway.

12.

Inside the warehouse, both men started loading the truck with the crates. Damn! Where was that backup! She had to stall them or soon they would drive off. This was too perfect to pass up, they had to contraband, and with all the men, she could probably get one or two to talk and-

-She froze as she felt the cold metal of a gun barrel pressed to the back of her neck.

"Freeze lady!" A shaky voice said, it sounded like a kid.

"I don't think you know who you're-" she started

"I... I said freeze!" Said the voice, bolder.

"Okay," She said and put her hands up. "I just want you to know that-"

"Shut up! Get up!" He said.

The gun was still pressed to her head. Felicia started to get to her feet. Looking back to the warehouse, she could see that the two men inside had stopped and were watching. She got to her feet and felt the gun move to her back.

"Move!" The kid said.

"Do you know how much trouble-"

"I said move!" His voice cracked as he shouted. Hands still in the air, Felicia walked forward. She kept her head high and tried to look tough... well as tough as she could with her ass hanging out.

She stepped into the warehouse, the teenage gun man on her back. Both of the men inside gaped at them.

"Jesus Travis, did you kidnap a supermodel or something?" One of them said.

"She's a cop and was spying on us!" He said.

"Ain't dressed like no cop!" The other said.

"I'm Sheriff Felicia Fetters, and all of you are under arrest." She said, head held high.

Both men exchanged a look and started laughing.

"Really?" One said, "Under arrest?"

"Yes," Felicia said, maybe if she stalled, back up would get here just in time. "Now I suggest you don't make this harder on yourselves."

The men laughed again.

"Boy Travis, this one's a riot." One of them said, "Take her out back to see Jack"

Jack! Janet mentioned a Jack! Fuck, she silently prayed for back up, if they could get Jack then this would be huge.

"You heard the man," Travis nudged her with the gun, "Move!"

She sighed and pressed forward, feeling the men's eyes on her as she moved.

"Nice pants, those standard issue?" One of the men said and she heard both laugh. Felicia kept her head held high. They wouldn't be laughing in a few minutes when the calvary arrived.

Travis ushered her through a door at the back of the warehouse and onto the dock. More men, at least a dozen, were loading and unloading crates from the boat. It had gotten chilly and she felt her ass cheeks once again break out in goosebumps.

"Cold huh?" Travis asked, snickering. Clearly he was looking at the hole in her pants.

"Staring at my ass? Enjoy it, I'll be kicking yours soon enough." She said.

A man stood in the center of the dock and turned to face them when he heard her voice. Like the others, he was clad all in black, complete with a black leather jacket. His black hair was spiked, and she could tell from his build that he worked out. He smiled when he saw them.

"Travis? What have you found here?" He said, eying Felicia up.

"I'm Sheriff Felicia Fetters, and all of you are under arrest." She said, making sure not to give Travis a chance to speak.

The man still smiled. "Is that so?"

"Yes." She said, listening for the sound of sirens, it should be any minute now.

"You must be that cute new Sheriff everyone is talking about." He started to move towards her. The man already knew who she was? Were people talking already? Or did Ace and his men keep that close tabs on the police situation? Worse, could someone in the department be working with them?

"And you must be Jack." She said. He shrugged as he moved towards her.

"Guilty as charged," he said, still smiling. His gaze shifted to Travis, "What are you staring at there Travis?"

Jack sauntered over and Travis stepped away. Felicia followed him to see that yes, he was just a kid, eighteen at the oldest, but big. He must have been a jock or something. Travis kept the gun trained on her as Jack circled her.

"Oh Sheriff Fetters, looks like you had a little accident there. You must be cold."

She said nothing and gritted her teeth. Jack circled back around to face her.

"Now Sheriff, we ain't hurting nobody, just moving some inventory."

"That inventory wouldn't happen to be guns?" She said and Jack's eyes widened. His jaw clenched, but then his smile was back after a second.

"Look Sheriff, Felicia, may I call you Felicia? There's a certain way things are around here, and since you're new, I'm going to cut you some slack. Turn around and go home and forget all about this, and

I'll forget this too. I can't promise to forget about seeing your sweet little ass but what red blooded American male would? So what do you say?"

She glared at him, ice in her eyes. "I have men on the way, if you give now then maybe we'll go easy on you."

Jack's smile disappeared. "We have to do something about those pants of yours, it's embarrassing to go around like that. Why don't you take them off."

Felicia still glared, her eyes full of fire. Jack took a gun from his pocket and leveled it at her while stepping back.

"I said, take them off. Actually, belt first. Then boots." He said, his smile returning.

Felicia turned, Travis had his gun trained on her too. Fuck, where was everyone? She turned back to Jack to see that the rest of the man had gathered around as well. With no other choice, she reached down and unclasped her gun belt.

"Travis, take the lady's things would you."

Travis ran over with hungry eyes. Felicia, still glaring, handed her gun belt over to the teen. He stepped back, never taking his eyes off of her. Next she squatted down for her boots, hearing another tear as her tights ripped even more. All of the men around giggled. Her fingers fumbled with the laces on the first boot, but she undid them and kicked it off, followed by the second one. She stood up to face Jack. Still no sirens.

"Your pants." He motioned with her gun. Felicia rolled her eyes and and gripped the waist band of her tights and slid them down. The men "ooohed" and yelped as they slid down past her already exposed ass to her thighs and then fell around her ankles. Once they were down, she stepped back and kicked them at Jack.

"There." She said, standing there half naked, raising her hands once again.

"Shirt now." He said.

She groaned, "You're just making this worse for yourself."

"No, you are." He said, "now, the shirt." Felicia sighed and started to unbutton her uniform shirt. Once it was undone, she slid it off her shoulders and let it fall to the ground. Now she stood in just her tank top. Instinctively she crossed her hands over her chest, trying to cover her near nudity.

"Uh-Uh," Jack leveled the gun at her, "Both shirts"

She sighed, "Seriously!"

"Yes!" he cocked the gun. "Seriously."

She let out another sigh and pulled off the beater, tossing it aside. Her eyes scanned the area to see where her clothes were. Once backup arrived, things would get crazy, and she wanted to gather her clothes and get dressed in the confusion.

"Travis, gather the Sheriff's clothes for us." Jack said.

Shit! She turned to watch Travis began scurrying around the dock, picking up her discarded items.

"Where's the packing tape?" Jack asked.

A henchman stepped forward, a roll of brown packing tape in hand. Felicia's eyes widened. Now would be a good time for her cops to arrive. Travis ran to Jack's side with Felicia's clothes and gun belt bundled in his arm.

"I got her stuff Jack." he said excitedly.

"Good," Jack said, "Toss it in the ocean."

Travis made off down the dock. Jack motioned the other henchman towards Felicia.

"Wrap up the Sheriff for me, will you?" He said.

Dammit no! She wasn't going to be tied up in her underwear and at the mercy of her goons.

"This is assaulting a police officer, my men are on their way and won't stand for this!" She shouted.

"Is that so?" Jack said. Meanwhile, the henchman stepped behind her and pulled both her arms behind her back. She tried to pull away but Jack aimed his gun at her, and she froze. The henchman crossed her wrists and she felt the sticky tape being wrapped around them. After a few layers, she felt him step away and she tried tugging. Her hands were taped tightly together.

"I swear, once I get out of this, I'll-"

"You're not getting out of this." Jack said smugly. The henchman's arms came from behind her. "What are you-" she started and felt the tape wrap around her body just below her breasts. She felt the tape wrap around her chest, to the back, get her arms, and come back around. In the end, several layers wrapped around her torso, pinning her arms to her back.

"Hey, let me go!" she screamed. Maybe there was someone passing by who would hear.

"You're a mouthy one, aren't you?"

167

"I'll get all of you for this!" She said. Meanwhile, the goon pulled her ankles together and wrapped several layers of tape around them. Felicia wobbled, trying to maintain her balance, but she didn't have to for long. Her captor came behind her, gripping both arms.

"Hey, get off me!" she screamed.

"Down!" he said, in a rough voice.

He succeeded in pushing Felicia into a sitting position, she grunted as she felt the rough, rotted wood of the dock dig into her bare ass cheeks. The man pulled her knees together and wrapped them in tape.

"Do you know much trouble you're in? I will throw every charge I can at you! You'll spend the rest of your life in jail! I'll-"

"Please, shut this bitch up!" Jack said through gritted teeth.

Felicia's eyes widened. No!

"Wait! No! I'll-UMMMMPH!"

A strip of tape was pulled between her gaping lips. Her tongue danced over the sticky substance and Felicia let out a squeal.

"GLLLUMMMPH!" She moaned as the henchman pulled the tape around her head. He grasped her chin with one hand, holding her steady while he wrapped, piling on the layers around her mouth.

"MMMMMMMPH! UMMMMMPH! LLMMMMMPPPH!"

The henchman ripped off the rest of the tape and stepped back to admire her. The entire lower half of her face was covered in brown packing tape, effectively gagging her.

"FLLLLLMUUMMPH! GGRRRRRGGGLE!" She moaned, trying to move her mouth, but the layers of tape kept her lips sealed tight.

"Ah, the sounds of silence." Jack said, walking over to her.

"Ulllllmmmph!" She twisted her head, trying to shake off the tape. Jack kneeled in front of her.

"Hey, look at me." he said.

"Mmmmmllluupph!" She rubbed her face on her elbow, hoping it would pull down the tape.

"I said look at me!"

"GRRRRRMMMMPH!" She groaned and shot her head up to face him, eyes blazing.

"You got spirit, I'll give you that. Now, I'm feeling charitable, I could just have my men toss you in the ocean-"

"UMMPH!" Her eyes widened.

"But, I won't. I'm going to send you on a cruise, a nice ride out of her, and wherever you end up, don't come back here. You here me? Forget about Marston's Pointe, live a nice life anywhere else, are we clear?"

"GRRRR" She growled through the gag and narrowed her eyes.

Jack sighed and rubbed his eyes.

"Where's this boat going after this?" He asked one of his goons.

"Not sure boss." someone answered. Jack turned back to her.

"Pack her away in one of the crates, have them unload her somewhere on their next stop. Someplace public, where someone will be able to hear her thrashing around inside."

"UMMMMMPH! NNNNNNOOOOO! MMMMMOOOO!" She shook her head, screaming into her gag. Rough hands seized her under the armpits.

"Sorry," Jack said, shrugging as she stood up, "I gave you a chance."

"Ullllmmmm mmoooo!" She moaned as another goon grabbed her by her tied feet. Both lifted her and she thrashed in their arms as they carried her down the docks.

"Ummmph! Mlllllmmmummmmlllpph! Mmmmlllllpppp!"

She twisted her head to see a wooden crate lying on it's back a few feet away. It's lid was off and resting near it, the open crate looked like a gaping mouth. Her eyes widened and she knew it waited for her.

"UMMMMMMPH! MMMMMMMOOOO! MMMMMMOOOH! OOOOLLLLLMMMPH!" She kicked and struggled as much as she could, forgetting her near nudity, forgetting about the back up that supposedly was coming.

Then they were there, hovering over the box. They lowered the struggling Sheriff inside. She barely fit, scrunching up into a ball in order to fully squeeze inside. Her knees were pressed up against her chest, her head tilted down towards her chest, and back pressed flat against the wood.

"GLLLLLUMMMP! MLLLLPPPRRRH!" She kicked against the

wood and turned her head to face her captors, now looming over her.

"Sorry Sheriff." One said and shrugged.

"GRRRRMMMPH! MMMLLLL FFFFETTTT MMMMMOOO

MMMMOORRRMMM GLLLLILLLMM" She screamed into her

gag and attempted to turn her scrunched body.

The henchmen disappeared but returned a second later with a length

of wooden held between, the top of the crate.

"MMMMOOOOO!" she shook her head, but it was no use. They

laid the top of the crate down, plunging her into darkness. Next she

heard the mechanical whir of a drill as screws were driven in place.

"MMMMMLLLLLMPPH! UMMMMMPH!" She rocked her body back and forth, but the crate held tight. Then she felt herself move as the crate was lifted.

"UMMMPPH!" She cried. Felicia shifted inside as she felt the crate being stood up, placing her body in a sitting position.

"GLLLLLUMMMPH!" She cried irritably.

Then she was moving again. She heard the grunt as the men carried the crate somewhere. The boat? Maybe, that had to be the only place. Unless they lied, unless they were going to dump her into the sea. Another jolt, and she felt herself get lifted even higher.

"LLLLLMMMMPH!" She complained and kicked the side of the crate.

She felt the crate set down again and another jolt went through her body and grunted into the gag. Now what? A boat ride to God Knows Where? No, she wasn't going down like this. Maybe if she rocked the crate hard enough, it would fall and break open. Then what? She would still have to escape the dozen or so armed men outside? Once again her plan came to just slowing them down, if she got loose, if even still taped, they would have to collect her and seal her in another crate, buying more time for-

-For what? Where the hell was that backup? And what would they think when they came and found the Sheriff, bound and gagged in her underwear? Public humiliation, that's what this was, either way. Just like in L.A...

Felicia shook her head, she had to swallow her pride, get out.

"GLLLLLLMMMPH! UMMMPH!" She moaned and started to rock her body back and forth. The crate shuttered and rocked around her. Yes!

Then she heard something outside. Raised voices. Shit, did they see her plan and come running to stop it. Felicia froze and listened. Yes, they were all yelling outside. But there was something else out there, another noise.

A police siren.

13.

"Hurry up! They're getting away!" Tanya shouted from the

passengers seat. James Randy just shook his head and tightened his

grip on the steering wheel. She hadn't shut up the entire ride to the

docks. He had been home, out of uniform and into a t-shirt and jeans,

and hadn't planned his night beyond looking up more photos of

Sheriff Fetters during her modeling days. Sheriff Fetters, wow, kinda uptight, but damn, was she something? The sight of Fetters' ass under those thin tights she was wearing had been burned into his brain.

Then he got the call from Deputy Cringe. There rarely was trouble in Marston's Pointe after dark, maybe a drunk or two, so the whole department had taken to going home, with the exception of Cringe, who manned the phones until 9 at least. After 9 Cringe left and closed up, and any call that came in would redirect to the private numbers of the Sheriff or Deputies. Apparently, Cringe was closing up shop when Tanya Donnelly called, frantic about some sort of trouble by the docks, and the Sheriff was involved. Randy got the call while in front of his computer, a photo of Felicia up, a beer in one hand, and his cock in the other. He downed his beer, buttoned up his jeans, and threw on his uniform shirt. He picked up Tanya a few blocks from the warehouse distract where she filled him in. An arms deal was going down, and Sheriff Fetters told Tanya to get help while she dealt with the men.

Randy was worried, Sheriff Fetters was going up against Ace's men alone, which was never a smart move.

"Hurry up!" Tanya screamed again as Randy drove down one of the narrow roads between warehouses, his siren blaring. Christ, Tanya was annoying. It seemed like every day she was in the station with a new theory or lead on Ace and his men, and the only reason Randy put up with it was because her tits were amazing. He heard that she liked to sunbathe in her back patio in tiny bikinis, and even though he always made a point on his patrols to pass her place, he had yet to have any luck in catching a glimpse of her.

He turned another corner and caught headlights heading in the opposite direction. "Oh no, they heard you! I told you not to put on the siren!" Tanya swatted at his shoulder. Randy ignored her and headed for the warehouse she described. There were at least four sets of headlights headed in the opposite direction down an access road that he knew lead to the highway.

Randy ignored the fleeing vehicles and took another turn. "What are you doing?" Tanya demanded.

He ignored her. If the bad guys were getting away, then where was the Sheriff? His palms were slick with sweat as he steered his cruiser came to a stop outside a small warehouse on the pier. Once parked, Randy killed the engine but left the lights on.

"No, they went the other way! Why are you stopping!" Tanya yelled.

"Tanya!" he started, then paused to catch his breath and collect himself. "Ms. Donnelly, we have to find the Sheriff first." He said through gritted teeth.

Tanya frowned and exited the vehicle. Randy followed her outside, his hand drifting to the gun on his hip. It was quiet, but the lights in the warehouse were still on and all of the doors open. They must have left in a hurry because a panel truck sat inside the warehouse by a loading bay with several large wooden crates stacked next to it.

Tanya strolled in, a small digital camera in her hands, and started snapping photos.

"Hey, can't do that!" Randy followed after her.

"Freedom of the press!" She said, still taking pictures. To be honest, Randy wasn't sure if she was allowed to take photos or not, but he decided that he didn't feel like arguing.

"Sheriff! Sheriff Fetters!" He shouted, but the warehouse was silent. Randy started to fear the worst, did they take her with them? A bay door was open leading to the outside and Tanya stepped out, Randy followed. On the ocean he could see the lights of a boat in the distance as it sailed away. More wooden crates were stacked on the edge of the dock.

Tanya snapped more photos as Randy surveyed the scene. Where was the Sheriff?

"Sheriff! Sheriff Fetters!"

"UMMMMPH! HLLLEEEEPPPH! MMMLLLEEELLPPH!" Muffled cries rose over the sound of the waves. Randy followed the sound and noticed a wooden crate sitting vertically on top of the other crates, and this crate was shaking back and forth. Someone was struggling inside!

Randy ran over. "Sheriff," he asked, "Are you in there?"

"GLLLLLUMMMPH! MMMMMPHHH!" was the muffled answer. The crate continued to rock back and forth as Felicia thrashed around inside. Tanya ran over, camera in hand. Randy gripped the edge of the box and noticed that it was screwed shut.

"Hold on Sheriff, I'm going to get you out of there!"

"UUMMM UMMMPH! LLLLUMMPPH!" was the reply.

Randy's eyes raced over the dock, looking for something to get the box open. Tanya ran over a second later with a crowbar. He took it and nodded in thanks.

"Hang on, we'll have you out in a minute!"

"MMMMMPH!"

Randy placed the crowbar under the seams of the crate and pried. The wood creaked and groaned as the screws worked free. Tanya stepped behind him, raising her camera. After a few moments, the front of the crate fell away, exposing what was inside. He stepped back and his jaw dropped.

"GLLLLLMMMPH!" The Sheriff glared at him, fury in her eyes. She was bound with brown packing tape, several layers of it covering the lower half of her face, gagging her. It also looked like the Sheriff was naked. Behind Randy, Tanya started snapping photos.

"UMMMMPH! UMMMPH!" Felicia mumbled and motioned at Randy with her head. After another moment, he noticed that she wasn't naked, but clad in a white sports bra and thong, the very same thong he had seem through her thin tights earlier that day.

"UMMMMPH!" She screamed under the gag, her eyes wide with fury.

Randy shook his head, "Uh, yeah Sheriff. I'll have you out of that in a minute." he said and stepped over to her.

"Ulllummmmph!" She mumbled in defeat and hung her head as Randy stepped over to the bound Sheriff. Meanwhile, Tanya continued to snap photos.

14.

Felicia woke up the next morning to the sound of the ocean outside and the sun shining through her bedroom windows. For one blissful moment she had forgotten about the previous night, but as she opened her eyes, it all came flooding back: being stripped of her clothes, being bound and gagged, locked in the crate, Deputy Randy finding her...

She groaned and sat up, completely naked. After Randy and Tanya had broken open the box, they quickly freed Felicia from the tape. Randy couldn't take his eyes off her half naked body, and Tanya had lent her the jacket she wore, though it only covered Felicia's upper body. EMTS had checked her out and she was relatively fine, mostly just angry and embarrassed. The goons left in a hurry, and Randy volunteered to take the weapons they left behind to evidence lock up after driving Tanya and Felicia home. Felicia had gone straight into her house and showered for close to an hour, and after had climbed

right into bed. Now she tossed aside the covers and stood up, looking

out her two windows that overlooked the beach. If anyone happened

to be passing outside then they would have been given a terrific view

of Felicia's tan, toned, naked body. Staring out the window, she was

thankful for how desolate the beach was, and also realized that she

should get blinds and curtains for her windows soon.

She took a quick shower and got dressed, this time wearing spandex

tights over a black thong. Thankfully she had another uniform shirt,

which she wore over a black sports bra, but she didn't have a second

gun belt, or gun for that matter. Felicia gritted her teeth, those men

would pay, dearly. Once she caught them, it would be the maximum

sentences for all of them, including that Jack. It was her mission now

to see Jack rot in a cell for the rest of his life.

The birds were singing as she stepped out onto her front porch, ready

to face the day, and the rest of her police department. She would acknowledge what happened, thank Deputy Randy for his help, and state that it would never happen again, and she meant it too. Felicia locked her door and turned to her driveway when a rolled up newspaper on the porch caught her eye. Strange, she didn't remember subscribing to the local paper, maybe the previous resident of the house did? The newspaper was called *The Marston Observer*, and Felicia picked it up and unrolled it.

Her jaw dropped when she saw the front page.

The front page was a photo of her from the previous night, packed in the crate, bound, gagged, and in her underwear. Her eyes were wide and pleading as they faced the photographer, Tanya. Above the photo was the headline "Bimbo Botches Beach Bust".

Felicia felt her blood turn to fire as she crumbled the newspaper in her hands. Tanya! That bitch! Her hands worked the paper into a tight wad and she tossed it at Tanya's house as she stormed towards her cruiser. Somehow, someway, Felicia would get Tanya for this public humiliation.

And that's exactly what this was, public humiliation, but for what? Why would Tanya do it? It occurred to Felicia that she should have read the article before crumbling up the paper, but now it was too late. She was supposed to be the Sheriff, but now there was a photo of her bound, gagged, and in her lingerie plastered all over town. She needed a quick rebound from this, somehow. Felicia needed to show strength, that she was a force to be reckoned with.

She had to bring in Ace, or Jack. It was time to show that she ran this town.

Things were not better when she got to the station. When she walked in the door the first thing she saw was Deputy Frank shoving the newspaper under his desk, his face beet red.

"What was that?" She asked, hands on her hips.

"Nothing." He said, crossing his hands in front of him.

"Nothing?" She asked, eyebrows raised.

"Nothing." was his response. Felicia sighed and turned around to see Alice sitting at her desk, paper open in front of her, the photo of Felicia's bound and gagged underwear clad form stared back at her, almost mocking. Her fists clenched and Felicia stalked over to the dispatcher's desk and ripped the paper out of the old woman's hands. Alice cried out and groped for the paper like a child reaching for her pacifier. Their eyes met, and Felicia never broke contact as she crumbled up the paper and tossed it in a garbage can.

"I was reading that!" Alice cried out.

"You're on duty, you can read when you get home." She turned to face the rest of her men, "Next person I see with that newspaper turns in their badge."

The air was tense, everyone stared, waiting on her next word.

"Is that clear?" Still no response.

"I said, is that clear!" She shouted, feeling the blood rush to her face. Everyone nodded back at her in agreement. "Deputy Randy!" she shouted.

James stepped forward, a styrofoam cup of coffee in hand.

"Yes?" His eyes were wide, afraid.

"My office." She barked and turned towards the room at the back of the station.

When she looked at the closed door to her office her eyes widened and she could feel her blood start to boil in her veins. Her fists and jaw clenched in the same moment. A small, pink and white bikini was pinned to the door, there was a note hanging on the bikini top, though she was too far to read the writing. Felicia strode forward, dimly aware of the pain in the palm of her hands from her fingernails digging in.

As she got closer to the bikini she could make out more details. The bikini top was pink with frilly white trim around the edges, and the bottom was nothing more than a small, pink g-string. The note hanging from the bikini top read: "Stop playing cops and robbers and go back to the beach". Her eyes scanned the note a few times and she felt her boiling blood turn to ice. Felicia whirled around to face the rest of the officers, whose eyes were wide and on her, jaws slack.

"Who did this?" She demanded. No one said anything.

"I want to know who did this. Speak up!" Still no one responded.

"No one wants to take responsibility? You think this is funny?" The tension in the room could be cut with a knife.

"If no one steps forward then I'll suspend you all without pay!"

"Come on Sheriff," Randy put a hand on her shoulder. "No one did it."

She pulled away and glared at him.

"No one? None of you did it?"

"It was..." Frank spoke up and then choked when Felicia focused on him. "It was... here when we got here."

"Really? And none of you felt the need to say anything or take it down?" Felicia placed her hands on her hips.

"N-n-n-no. We didn't know what to do, and then when you came in and were in a bad mood we didn't...." Frank swallowed and looked down. Felicia looked at him and then back to Randy.

"You expect me to believe that someone just came in and put this here?"

"You gotta believe us Sheriff, none of us did it." Randy pleaded.

Felicia bit her lip. If it wasn't one of her men then it meant that someone else was trying to send a message to her, Ace? Maybe, it didn't take Randy long to find out about her modeling days, so it would make sense for Ace to do the same. She stormed towards the door and ripped the bikini down.

"Randy, inside now." She barked.

They entered her office and she slammed the door behind them, tossing the bikini and note onto her desk. Randy, shaky cup of coffee still in hand, took a seat as Felicia sat behind her desk.

"The guns, where are they?"

"Evidence lockup," he responded, still shaking.

"And what did we find on them?" She eyed him.

"Nothing." He said, avoiding her gaze.

"Nothing?" she asked.

"There's no manifest or paperwork on the guns, no prints, the serial numbers are filed off... we have nothing."

Her fists clenched and she leaned forward, "I have Jack on the scene."

"I... no one knows where to find him, or his men. We have nothing to connect them to Ace..." He trailed off, waiting for her reaction.

Felicia leaned back, doing her best to mask her frustration.

"Maybe if we talked to Tanya about her source, they could-" he began before she cut him off.

"No!" She blurted out, causing Randy to jump and spill coffee all over his hand. He cried out and used his other sleeve to wipe the drink away.

Felicia got a grip on herself and stared up at him.

"No, I will not bring that woman in on this investigation. Is that clear?"

Randy nodded.

"Dismissed." She said and he scampered away. Felicia watched him go and leaned back, letting out a groan. Jesus, this was only day two. Outside, Randy took his seat at his desk, exchanging a nervous look with Frank. It suddenly dawned on Felicia that she didn't want to spend any more time in this office, or building. She had to get out... somewhere, just drive or... or something. Her eyes fell on the bikini on her desk and her blood boiled again.

Felicia got to her feet, snatched the bikini off of her desk, and headed for the exit. All eyes turned to her as she exited her office.

"If you need me, get me on the radio." She said and pushed through the main doors and out into the beautiful morning sun.

15.

Thankfully, Felicia found that Rossi's was open, a thick wooden board was hammered in place where the broken glass once was. At first Felicia didn't really know why she went to Rossi's, but then realized that she didn't really know where else go other than back home, and if so then she might run into Tanya, and if she ran into Tanya now... then God help that woman. Janet was working the bar and gave Felicia a look of surprise when she took a seat.

Janet was dressed far more appropriately than the last time they met, and was wearing tight blue jeans and a white tank top that showed off her magnificent breasts perfectly. Felicia tried not to stare when she ordered a beer.

"Drinking on duty?" Janet raised an eyebrow under her glasses.

"Been that kind of day." Felicia answered.

Janet nodded and went over to her tap.

"I saw the paper today, I'm... sorry to hear about what happened. I'm glad to see that you're okay though."

Felicia nodded as Janet handed her a sweating glass filled with amber liquid.

"I met our friend Jack." She said. Janet's eyes widened.

"Look, these guys, they're... tough customers. Maybe take it easy for a while." Janet said.

Felicia shook her head.

"I can't take this lying down. They humiliated me. Not to mention that they'll keep coming for your bar. Next time they may do more than break a window."

Janet sighed and leaned forward, her arms pushing her tan breasts together nicely, and giving Felicia an excellent view.

"Look, I'm thinking of getting out," Janet said. "This town, it's going to Hell, and Ace and his boys won't stop. You seem like a good kid, maybe you should get out too."

Felicia shook her head.

"I'm not running away. I promise you that I will save your bar and put Ace and his boys behind bars."

"But you can't do it by yourself." Janet stood back up, but her eyes never left Felicia.

"No, no I can't." Felicia admitted.

"I like you, I know I was rude the other day, but... I think you mean well. I just don't want to see you tied up in my newspaper again, or worse."

"Don't worry," Felicia smiled. "I don't intend on letting anyone tie me up again."

16.

Felicia finished her drink and decided to head home, thinking that maybe some time on the beach may help her relax. Yes, that would do it. She would dig out one of her bikinis, maybe take a quick dip, and then relax in the sun. As she drove, she looked over at the string bikini on the seat next to her. Why was she keeping it when she should have just tossed it in the garbage and not given it a second thought? But she knew why, deep down it was because of her vanity. Some part of her thought that she would look good in that bikini, if it even fit. And so what if it fit? What better way to show that the taunts didn't work then by flaunting it in her tormentors face? Especially if she did look good in that bikini.

As Felicia pulled into her driveway, her eyes widened when she noticed Tanya getting out of her car. Damn! She was hoping to avoid her. Tanya saw Felicia's cruiser parking and her eyes widened. Felicia parked and sighed, hoping that Tanya would have the good sense to go inside.

She didn't. Tanya stepped into her front yard and waited, hands on her hips. Felicia glared at her from inside the car, but then figured that she may as well get this over with. The sound of the ocean greeted her as she stepped out of her cruiser and locked eyes with Tanya.

"Mrs. Donnelly." Felicia nodded.

"Ms. Donnelly." Tanya corrected.

209

"Fine," Felicia said and stepped into her yard, a fence keeping her and Tanya apart. "So I saw your piece in the paper."

"Thank you," Tanya said, hands still on her hips. "It's been a big seller."

"I have no doubt." Felicia stopped at her fence and met Tanya's gaze. "Those were pictures of a crime scene and you had no right to publish them."

"Well, you should have spoke up, said something." Tanya smiled.

"I was having difficulty communicating at the time," Felicia grimaced. "Next time you pull anything like that again, I will shut your little paper down."

Tanya glared at her.

"You wouldn't dare." She said, her eyes narrowing.

"Try me." Felicia said through gritted teeth.

"If you would have just stayed out of all of this then everything would be alright, and I wouldn't have posted your incompetence up for the world to see." Tanya clamped her hands on hips, her face turning as red as her hair.

"What? Mind my own- Listen, if I wouldn't have gotten involved then it would have been you taped up in that box!"

Tanya snorted. "I had a plan! I would have gotten photos, clear shots of Jack and Ace's men bringing in weapons, that would have been enough to get the Feds involved!"

"What... what are you talking about?" Felicia stammered. Feds? FBI? What was Tanya on about?

"Forget it!" Tanya threw her hands up in exasperation. "You don't get it, no one does! Ace is going to keep running rampart through this town, and you had to go in half cocked and scare off his men. We need more good men like Sheriff Vorhees!" The woman's face was a deep scarlet now and she spun around and stormed towards her house.

"Next time, don't follow me!" She screamed and ripped open her front door.

"If I catch you at a crime scene again, I'll toss your ass in jail!"
Felicia screamed after her.

Tanya slammed her door behind her. Felicia unclenched her own
fists and realized that she was shaking. Who the hell did this woman
think she was, Nancy Drew? She probably saved Tanya's life last
night and this is how she re-payed her? Forget it, Felicia would find
a way to take care of Tanya, somehow.

She sighed and turned towards her front door, it was time to change
and go for a dip in the ocean.

"Oh that Tanya, what a fiery temper she has. Means well though."
Felicia heard a female voice behind her. She turned around to see a
thin blond woman standing on the sidewalk watching her. The
woman was dressed for business, with a very short, black pencil skirt
that showed a lot of leg, and a black button down shirt with the top

few buttons open. Her breasts were small but pushed up to show nice cleavage under the shirt, and she wore a black blazer over the shirt. Felicia eyed the woman up, she was thin but very toned, a dancer's body, and she would bet any money that this woman had a great ass.

"I'm sorry?" Felicia asked. The woman smiled and stepped towards Felicia's fence. Her blond hair stopped just short of her shoulders and blew in the ocean breeze.

"Shelly Arnold." She smiled and extended a hand. Felicia stepped towards the fence and shook it.

"Nice to meet you." Felicia broke off the shake.

"How have you been settling in? Sounds like things have been difficult so far." Shelly asked, still smiling.

"It's been bumpy but I'll manage, now if you'll excuse me." Felicia nodded and turned back to her house, not in the mood for small talk.

"Sheriff, I was wondering if you wanted to stop by my place for a drink, I have something to discuss with you." Shelly's tone was very business like.

"Perhaps another time." Felicia said, stepping towards her door.

"I promise that I'll make it worth your while." Shelly called. Felicia stopped and looked back, Shelly was smiling.

"I hate to be pushy, but it concerns matters that are of great importance to you, me, and this town as a whole." Shelly watched Felicia with inquisitive eyes.

"Tanya doesn't seem to be the biggest fan of you." Felicia asked, remembering that Tanya said that Shelly was a "Backstabbing bitch".

"Tanya sees enemies in every corner, but I assure you that we all want the same thing. I just hope that you're more reasonable than her."

Felicia looked at her house, listening to the sounds of the ocean beyond, and turned back to Shelly.

"Five minutes." She said.

Shelly's smile got even bigger.

17.

Felicia's brow furrowed in confusion at the photo in her hand. It was

taken at night, the photographer was shooting through a window

from the outside. Through the window, Felicia recognized Tanya,

wearing a black bra and a short, black, see through teddy. The teddy

stopped just above Tanya's ass, where she wore a tiny, black thong.

Tanya's back was to the window but Felicia recognized her from the red hair and from her plump ass cheeks. Inside the room with Tanya was a man, maybe middle-aged judging from the grey streaks in his brown hair. The man was stretched out on a bed, and wore a brown police uniform shirt similar to Felicia's. Flipping through the rest of the photos, they only got much more... explicit.

She tossed the photos down on a table. Shelly had invited Felicia into her home and brought her down to her basement, which is where Felicia guessed Shelly had done most of her entertaining. The basement had a huge flatscreen tv set up against a far wall, a full bar at the other end, and a large, jacuzzi right in the middle. At first Shelly offered Felicia a drink, which she refused, and then Shelly handed her an envelope. After handing off the envelope, Shelly excused herself upstairs while Felicia flipped through it.

Seconds after tossing the photos down, Felicia heard the basement door open and Shelly make her way down. It looked like Shelly had changed out of her business suit into something much more... casual.

Her blond hair was pulled back into a ponytail and she wore a thin, black robe that stopped right at her thighs. Though the robe was tied at the waist, Felicia could see that Shelly wore what looked like a black bikini underneath.

"What are these?" Felicia asked, motioning to the photos. What was Shelly's game?

"That man is Wilson Vorhees, recognize the name?" She smiled and stepped over to the jacuzzi, flipping it on. The calm water started to churn and bubble.

"Sheriff Vorhees." Felicia nodded.

"He and Tanya were... intimate, but he was also a married man. Like you, he swore to clean up this town, and by doing so painted a target on his back."

"Are you threatening me? Did you take these photos?" Felicia demanded.

Shelly's draw dropped and a hand went to her chest.

"Oh heavens no! I would never. It took me some time to gain possession of these photos." Shelly took at seat at the edge of the jacuzzi.

"Care to join me for a dip?" She asked.

"I don't think I have the appropriate attire" Felicia responded, watching Shelly.

Shelly smiled and started undoing the robe.

"I would let your borrow a spare bikini of mine, but I fear they won't fit you. You can go in naked, I won't mind." She smiled as the robe fell open, exposing her small but firm breasts being held up by a black string bikini top. Shelly turned around and let the robe drop, showing that she wore black, thong bikini bottoms.

Felicia's assumption earlier was right, Shelly did have a magnificent ass, and it fed into great legs, and that thong accented both perfectly. Her back still towards Felicia, Shelly leaned over, draping her robe over the edge of the jacuzzi, and drifted a hand over the churning waters.

"Ace had his men take those photos, and threatened to show them to Vorhees' family, spread them around town, discredit both he and Tanya unless Vorhees stepped down."

"So he did." Felicia finished, and Shelly turned back to face her and nodded.

"Since then, Tanya's been obsessed with taking down Ace, thinking that if she does so then Wilson will come back."

"How do you play into all this?" Felicia asked. Shelly had to have an angle.

"I'm just a concerned citizen that wants her son to grow up in a safe place. Tanya disapproves of my methods because I'm close to Ace's organization, but it's the best way to get information. Keep your enemies close."

"Were you her source? About the shipment last night?" Felicia asked, and Shelly nodded.

" I had to inform her anonymously of course, she would never trust it coming from my mouth. It's a shame things went the way it did, but I should have known that she would botch it. She's too close to all of this, wants it too much."

"So what do you want with me?" Felicia was on edge, it was hard to tell what Shelly wanted, especially if she played both sides like she was implying.

"You're two days in, and already have been the subject of a major embarrassment, Ace and his men have fired the first shot and scored a hit."

"Get to the point." Felicia sighed.

"Jack is the eyes and ears of Ace, his man on the street. He knows everything about how the operation is run, to get him would be a boon, and a way to redeem yourself in the eyes of this town and the police."

"And?" Felicia asked. So far, Shelly was telling her everything she already knew.

"What if I could give him to you?"

Felicia's jaw dropped. "Jack? You know where he is?"

Shelly smiled and nodded. "Ace and his men have safe houses all over town, I have it on good information that Jack will be at one tonight. Despite all that happened, you did wound them by taking their weapons. Jack and company will be planning their next move."

"Where are they?" Felicia could feel her blood pumping, this could be huge, her chance to strike at this organization and-

-Wait, how could she trust this woman? This could all be a set up, for all she knew, Shelly could be working for Ace.

"How do I know that I can trust you?" She asked.

"Go to the address I'm going to give you, tonight, and see for yourself. I know that it's a hard pill to swallow, but I want to help. You don't have to make a move tonight, but it's a good opportunity to stake them out and plan your next move."

"I don't need you to tell me how to do my job."

"Of course, my apologies. Take this as a sign of good faith, I hope that we can continue to work with each other after this."

Felicia looked at Shelly, and then that newspaper article flashed through her mind, the photo of her bound and gagged on the front page...

She had to do something. Felicia decided that she would trust this woman. Over By the jacuzzi, Shelly smiled and stepped in, keeping her back to Felicia the whole time.

"Care to join me?" She settled down, and leaned back, watching Felicia with hungry eyes. Felicia looked up and met Shelly's gaze.

"Where do I go?"

Shelly smiled and stared at the Sheriff.

"Why don't you step for a dip with me? Then we'll talk."

Felicia sighed and balled her fists.

"I don't have time for this. Tell me where to go."

Shelly wagged a finger at Felicia in a "tsk tsk" motion.

"Uh uh, that isn't how this is played. Come on in, join me, and I'll tell you what I want to know."

Felicia bit her lip and fumed. Was this woman trying to seduce her? Everything about this seemed like that. Inside the jacuzzi, Shelly continued to smile at the Sheriff.

"The heat gets to me, I'll be getting out any minute now." She cooed.

"Fine, I'll join you for a dip." Felicia said.

Shelly took a position against the back of the jacuzzi, spread her arms, and watched as Felicia kicked off her boots. After that, her fingers worked along the buttons of her shirt. The top few buttons came undone, exposing her bra and cleavage. From the hot tub, Shelly's eyes widened with amusement.

Felicia finished unbuttoning her shirt and shrugged it off. Then she gripped the waist band of her tights and slid them off as fast as she could. The last thing she wanted to do was give this woman a show.

Now clad only in her bra and thong, Felicia took a few steps towards the jacuzzi.

"Uh uh, you're not going to step in here in your underwear are you? It will be all wet for the rest of the night."

Felicia glared at Shelly.

"I'm not undressing any more. This is how you get me."

Shelly sighed and stood up.

"Then I'm afraid we're done here." She started heading for the other side of the hot tub.

"Wait!" Felicia stepped forward. Shelly stopped and stared, eyes wide.

"What I see here doesn't leave this room. I need to know if I can trust you, Sheriff. Show me that and I'll show you that you can trust me." Shelly sat back down in the hot tub.

Felicia sighed. She could just gather up her clothes and leave, but what then? She would be back at square one, with no leads on Ace. But what if Shelly didn't know anything? What if she was just playing Felicia?

"I'm waiting Sheriff." Shelly said.

Fine, Felicia decided to take the risk. She reached behind her back and undid the clasp on her bra. Shelly watched with rapt attention as Felicia tossed the undergarment aside, exposing her bare breasts to the woman. Next she slid off her panties and stood before the woman, fully nude.

Shelly's hungry eyes ran over Felicia's nude body.

"You have an excellent body Sheriff.

Felicia's hands instinctively moved to cover her bare breasts.

"Nope, we have no secrets here." Shelly said.

Felicia let her hands drop and moved towards the jacuzzi.

"Come in, the water's fine." Shelly said, leaning back.

Felicia walked up the few stairs leading to the hot tub and set one foot in. The water was warm and inviting. She set her other foot in and stepped into the bubbling waters of the tub. Shelly leaned back and watched.

Felicia made her way over to a seat and lowered herself down, feeling the jets of warm water rub against the muscles of her back and bare ass.

"Lean back, relax Sheriff, you look like you need it."

Felicia set her head back in the seat and felt the jets of the tub on her body. It felt amazing and she realized she did need it. From across the tub, Shelly continued to watch.

"How does it feel?" She asked.

"Amazing." Felicia responded.

Shelly smiled.

"Relax Sheriff, take it in. I love nothing more than coming down here after a long day, taking my clothes off, and blowing off a little steam." Shelly cooed. Felicia felt the waters of the tub shift and noticed that Shelly was sidling over towards her.

Felicia sat up and watched as the woman stopped and hovered just across from her.

"So, tell me what you know." Felicia demanded.

Shelly smiled and moved towards the Sheriff, they were both face to face.

"Now now Sheriff, if I'm going to do something for you then you have to do something for me."

Felicia gritted her teeth and stared at Shelly. This was a power play.

"What do you want?" Felicia asked.

Shelly stood up, towering over the Sheriff, and then reached up and started untying the bikini top. A moment later, the black bikini top fell away into the tub and Shelly stood with her small breasts exposed.

"Hey!" Felicia shot up but Shelly reached out, grabbed both of her shoulders, and with surprising strength pushed the Sheriff back down. The Sheriff felt her ass bounce off of the seat in the hot tub as she glared up at Shelly.

"What are you gonna do for me Sheriff?" Shelly grabbed the straps on either side of her bikini bottoms and slid the skimpy thong down. The discarded bikini bottoms floated in the tub next to the bikini top and Shelly stood completely nude in front of the Sheriff.

Felicia leaned back and swallowed, not liking where this was going. Shelly leaned over, her bare breasts right in Felicia's face.

Hey, wait..." Felicia leaned her head back as Shelly settled in, leaning forward to straddle the Sheriff.

Then Shelly forced herself down and under the surface of the tub Felicia could feel the woman's bare, shaved crotch rub against hers. Shelly pushed forward, her breasts pressed against Felicia's breasts.

"Shelly, tell me-"Shelly pressed a finger over Felicia's lips.

"I need to know that I can trust you. Make me tell you."

Felicia clenched her jaw and pulled away from the shushing finger.

"I'll come back with a court order-ummmph!" The finger over her lips turned into the full palm of Shelly's hand, cupped over Felicia's mouth.

"Come on Sheriff, you can do better than that. If you can't make me, someone who wants to help you, talk, then how can you make Jack talk?"

"Ummmm..." Felicia growled into Shelly's hands and glared up at the woman. This game was getting tiring.

Shelly removed her hand from Felicia's mouth and sat up, staring down at the Sheriff. Felicia flashed her a defiant stare and Shelly nodded.

"Tell me what you know." Felicia demanded.

Still straddling the Sheriff, Shelly reached over to her robe, still draped over the end of the tub, and pulled at it. Once she had the robe in her grasp, she pulled the black sash out of the loop in the back and then tossed the rest of the robe away. The sash was long and made of black satin, and Shelly held it out in front of her with both hands.

Felicia's eyes widened and she suspected what Shelly was going to do with it.

"Hey, don't think about it!" She warned, eyes narrowing, her blood turning to ice.

Shelly shook her head.

"It's not for you. I'm not going to speak until you do something for me."

With that, Shelly pulled the sash up, pressed it in her mouth between her teeth, and started tying it at the back of her neck.

"Hey, wait!" Felicia groped at Shelly, but the woman swatted the Sheriff's hands away. Annoyed, Felicia rolled her eyes and reached to pull down the gag again, but Shelly grabbed both her hands by the wrist and forced them down.

Felicia's jaw dropped and once again she was stunned at how surprisingly strong this thin woman was. She tried to pull her hands free but Shelly had them in a vice like grip. Their eyes met.

"Hummmm...." Shelly cooed into her gag and pressed forward, her hands still wrapped around Felicia's wrists. Felicia leaned back as Shelly pressed forward and nuzzled her gagged mouth against Felicia's.

"Ummmm...mmmmm..." Shelly cooed, rubbing her bare crotch against Felicia's.

"Shelly, tell me..." Felicia started.

"Ummm mmmm ummm" Shelly moaned. She had yet to release her grip on Felicia's hands and was now pulling Felicia's hands towards her. Felicia tried to resist and pull her hands back but suddenly her hands burst into pain as Shelly tightened her grip, digging her fingers into the pressure points on the wrist.

Felicia cried out and gave in, letting Shelly have complete control. The other woman leaned forward, rubbing her bare breasts against Felicia's and moved both of the Sheriff's hands up her slender thighs, along her hips, and finally to Shelly's sculpted buttocks. As she did this, Shelly continued to rub her crotch against Felicia's and moan into her gag.

"Ummmppp... mmmmppp.... ummm" Shelly moaned as she pressed Felicia's hands against her rear end. Felicia leaned back, closing her eyes.

She could feel the jets of warm water along her back, down her side, along her ass, each muscle releasing tension, easing itself. Shelly's body gyrated against her, her crotch rubbing up and down along Felicia's bare body. Their breasts bounced and heaved against each other. Felicia wanted to resist, to push this woman off her, to leave...

But it had been so long for her since she had been touched.

Shelly relaxed her grip on Felicia's hands, but still kept them pressed against her bare ass. Felicia was surprised by how tight and lithe Shelly's entire body was. She was a small woman, but a powerful one. Felicia wanted to know more- but no, she couldn't give in, she had to resist. Meanwhile, Shelly continued gyrating, pressing and thrusting against Felicia.

Felicia gave in and dug her nails into either of Shelly's butt cheeks. They were tight, solid all the way through.

"Urrrrmmm..." Shelly moaned and leaned her head back. She let go of Felicia's wrists and brought her hands around to the front, either one digging into Felicia's bare breasts.

Felicia leaned her head back and sighed as Shelly massaged her breasts, the lithe woman's arms squeezing and kneading. Shelly leaned forward and nuzzled Felicia again.

"Tell me... tell me..." Felicia sighed.

"Umm hmmm" Shelly shook her head. Felicia moved one of her hands away from the woman's butt cheek and along her waist to her thigh. Another moan of pleasure escaped Shelly's gagged lips.

"Ummhurrrmm." her whole body quaked.

243

Under the water, Felicia's hand snaked along Shelly's thigh to her bare crotch. The skin was just as smooth as the rest of her body. She moved her hand down, her finger dancing along the outer lips of Shelly's vagina.

"Ummm" Shelly moaned and ran her fingers through Felicia's hair. Felicia's fingers continued to trace the outside of Shelly's vagina. The woman continued to moan and shudder.

Then Felicia worked her fingers in and traced the very inside of Shelly's sex.

"Urrmmm! Mrrrrmm!" She gritted her teeth around her gag. Felicia's fingers worked faster now as they moved closer towards Shelly's clit. Shelly tightened her grip on Felicia's hair and pulled the Sheriff forward, burying the Sheriff's face in her heaving bosom.

"Urrmmm, mrrmm..." Shelly continued to moan.

Felicia's fingers found the woman's clit and danced along it, tracing wide circles as Shelly shuttered and convulsed.

"Urrrmm!" Shelly moaned, her entire body rocking.

Felicia looked up at the woman, her lips wrapped tightly around the gag, her eyes closed, head tilted back in pleasure. Then, Felicia raised her head and flicked her tongue over Shelly's erect, pink nipple. The woman continued to shudder and quake with excitement. Leaning forward, Felicia wrapped her lips around the woman's nipple and sucked.

"Ummmph!" Shelly ran her fingers through Felicia's thick hair. Under the surface of the hot tub, Felicia brought up her other hand to Shelly's crotch, raised one finger, and inserted it inside the gagged woman's moist vagina.

"Urrrmmph!" Shelly moaned, let go of Felicia's hair, reached up, and ran her hands through her own hair.

"Urrrmmp!" She cried, tussling her own hair.

Felicia smiled, knowing now that she had Shelly in the palm of her hand, and wiggled her finger inside the woman, all the while working her clit with the other hand.

"Mmmmmmmph!" Shelly cried, and her entire body convulsed as Felicia felt her come. She tossed her hair back and reached both arms out to her side, fists clenched as a final quake went through her body.

"Grrrlllumm..." Shelly let out something that sounded like a giggle, then collapsed into the tub opposite of Felicia. Shelly was now seemingly in a daze, her eyes closed and her lips twisted in something like a small around the gag. The Sheriff grabbed the satin gag and ripped it out of Shelly's mouth.

"Now, let's talk." She said, brushing her wet hair out of her face.

Shelly giggled and opened her eyes.

18.

Well, here I am, Felicia thought as she sat, ear pressed to the thick wooden door of the small apartment that she had a feeling would be her home for the night. Shelly had given her the address to an apartment complex on the outskirts of town, the part of town nobody talks about. As Felicia drove to the spot, she couldn't help but feel apprehension as she drove. Many of the homes had multiple junked cars rotting in the front yards. And there were far too many homes that were rotted and abandoned. Wisely, Felicia stopped at home first and left her police cruiser for her regular car, and now she could only imagine the looks some of these people would give a police car as it rolled through this section of town. There used to be businesses in this end of town as well, judging from the long boarded up overgrown storefronts.

The front door to the apartment building was locked but Shelly told Felicia that she could find two keys under a mat outside: One for the front door and one for Apartment 301. Shelly had told Felicia that Jack and his men conducted their business out of Apartment 302, directly across the hall. Of course all of this had set off warning bells in Felicia's head and she asked Shelly how she knew this and how she had these keys. Apparently, 301 was Shelly's apartment, for when she wanted to be "discreet". Felicia had a hard time imagining Shelly being more discreet than their hot tub encounter earlier.

So basically this was Shelly's love nest, and now Felicia was using it for a stakeout. The apartment itself was neatly furnished, with a couch, tv, tables, etc. It had a small kitchenette, a bedroom with a neatly made bed, bathroom with a fully stocked cabinet, and the fridge was fully stocked as well. This was an apartment meant for entertaining, not for living in. Felicia wondered how many men, or women, Shelly brought back here. She remembered Tanya mentioning that Shelly had a son, so maybe she brought company here for when they wanted to be alone? Either way, it wasn't a bad place for a stakeout, which usually involved Felicia being in her car or a cooped up van for hours on end.

So Felicia waited. She dived into apartment 301 quickly, not wanting to draw attention since she was still in uniform, and had taken up her position by the door, waiting and listening. The apartment across the hall, in fact the entire floor, maybe the entire building, was eerily quiet, but that was good, it would make it easier to listen when something did go down. Felicia didn't expect much, if anything, to happen tonight. Her plan was to wait and see if Shelly's story checked out, that Jack and Ace's men used this apartment as a safe house. If she could pick up any intel then that would be great, but she planned on this just being recon. If apartment 302 was a safe house, then she planned on eventually getting recording and surveillance equipment into 301 and getting any dirt she could. Shelly would have to find a new love nest.

Hours passed. The only time Felicia got up was to use the bathroom and considered putting on the tv but thought better of it, afraid the nose would alert someone if they heard it. More time passed and Felicia found herself pacing up and down in front of the door. This all could be a bust, hours wasted. Then what? Just go home, go back to the station in the morning and maybe find another bikini waiting. The bikini, she looked at it, draped over the back of the couch. Felicia had taken it out of her cruiser and thrown it inside her car, but when she got to the apartment building she had taken it with her, worried that a skimpy bikini sitting in a strange car might draw attention. Now she stared at it, getting drawn into the white trim on the top. It would look cute on her, wouldn't it?

No. She shook her head and looked out the peephole into the hallway. Still nothing, 302 sat quiet directly across from her. Felicia turned away and looked back at the bikini. If she was still modeling she could have done a killer beach shoot in that, but then again she didn't even know if it fit her. Her head turned to the doorway, it was still silent, then back to the bikini.

Fuck it! She shrugged, she had to pass the time somehow, plus she could change back into her uniform right after.

Felicia quickly stripped out of her uniform and then her underwear, tossing them in a heap onto the couch, and then slid into the bikini. It didn't just fit, it fit perfectly.

Too perfect. She frowned, looking down at her tan breasts heaving under the bikini top. How did they get her sizes? Maybe online? Being a former model, it was feasible that her measurements got online somehow.

The living room had a full length mirror mounted on a wall and Felicia stepped forward to admire herself. She looked great, stunning actually. The bikini top pushed her breasts up and in, giving her plenty of nice, heaving cleavage. The top was a bit small though, and the bottom of her breasts curved under the tiny top. As for the bottom well...

Felicia turned and admired her ass in the mirror. It wasn't a typical "T back" g-string, and instead the pink strings curved perfectly over each butt cheek and down into her crack, perfectly framing and accenting her rear end. It was hot, and a little too risque for a beach day. She turned back to her front and stuck her hand on her hip in a typical modeling pose. Damn, she still had it.

Voices in the hallway brought her back to the moment.

Shit!

She turned away from the mirror towards the door. Several voices, not loud, but conversational, and she recognized one of them: Jack.

Felicia ran to the couch to grab her uniform but heard a door open across the hall. Shit! She could get dressed later!

The bikini clad sheriff ran to the door and looked out the peephole. Jack held the door to 302 open while several men shuffled in. Here it is, go time! Once the last man was in, Jack looked around, and then followed them in, closing the door behind him. Felicia held her breath.

He didn't close the door all the way! Instead, he stopped it just shy of a full close. After another second, the door drifted open a bit, letting a little bit of light from the apartment spill out. Still holding her breath, Felicia stuck her ear against the door and listened. There were voices, but they were muffled, garbled. She strained, gripping her door handle, her chest growing tight...

Still nothing but garbled gibberish. Slowly she let out her breath, if only she could hear what they were saying!

But she could! Her eyes widened. If she was out in the hallway then she could definitely hear through the partially closed door, but what if they caught her? No, Jack thought he closed the door, so that gave her a few minutes, plus if she heard them coming towards the door, she could just slip back into 301. If she left her door open, then she could jump in and close her door before they even knew she was out there. That would be it then, just a quick listen, then back to the apartment.

Felicia stood straight, gripped her door handle, and started to turn it when she realized she was still in a bikini. Damn! A girl in a skimpy bikini listening at a door would definitely draw attention. She turned towards the couch where her clothes lie strewn when she heard raised voices outside. Turning back to the keyhole, she could see that the door to 302 was still slightly open, and someone was talking very loudly. Shit!

She turned back to her clothes, they would have to wait. It would be a quick pop into the hallway where she would assess the situation, and then back into the room. Felicia turned the door handle and stepped out into the hallway.

She let the door swing open behind her as she moved across the hall, and she couldn't help but feel exposed. If anyone came up the stairs or out of their apartments then they would get a face full of her almost bare ass. Felicia stopped just outside of 302 and crouched down by the door knob, listening.

"I mean shit dude, if we fuck this up, Ace will kill us right and good!" A voice said

"Don't worry, we'll be fine. Tonight will go off without a hitch, and then we'll get the guns back, and be back in Ace's good graces, it's all good." Said another voice, a voice she recognized as Jack's.

"The cops have the guns man, how are we going to deal with that?"

"Don't worry, I got someone on the inside." Jack said.

Felicia's eyes widened. Someone on the inside! One of her cops was working with Ace and Jack. Who could it be? Was that person the one that left the bikini?

As she mulled this over in her head, she didn't notice the footsteps approaching from behind. A shadow fell over Felicia and she gasped and stood up.

A rough, strong hand wrapped around her mouth.

"ULLLLLMMMMPH!" She screamed into the palm of her attacker. Another hand grabbed her arm and twisted it behind her back. Her free arm shot up and tried to pry the hand away from her mouth but whoever this was, he was strong, and his hand was clamped around her mouth like a vice.

"GLLLLMMMMOOO!" She gurgled as the man pushed her forward and kicked the door open with a strong kick.

She fought and pushed back as the much stronger man forced her inside, his hand stifling her protests.

"ULLLLLMMMM! MMMMMM! UMMMM-LLLMMM-GLLLLMMMM!" Her eyes widened as she was forced inside the apartment. Everyone inside was standing in a circle, but all froze when Felicia was forced inside. Their eyes widened to saucers when they saw what Felicia was wearing.

"MMMMM-UULLLMMMM-GLLLLUMMPH!" She fought as her captor forced her closer to the group. Jack approached, a smile on his face.

"Well, if it isn't our cute little Sheriff. Did you miss me that bad?"

"Grrrmmmmph!" She spit into the hand that silenced her.

"And you even wore your best for me?" Jack's greedy eyes traced the curves of her body. Felicia let out a mumble and shot a leg out to kick him but he backed away.

"I caught her listening at the door boss." Said her captor.

"It seems we can't get rid of you." Jack said, his eyes meeting hers.

"Ummmmph!" She kicked again, her bare leg flailing in the air.

"I was nice last time, I even gave you a warning. I won't be so kind this time."

"Mmmmmmmrrrrrppph!"

"Take her out to the car and keep her quiet. I think I know what to do with her."

"Sure boss." The goon started to drag her away, and Felicia started to fight and kick.

"Ummmmph! Mmmm-lllummmph! Lllllleeeelllmmmmph! Lllllmmmmph!"

But her struggles were useless. Whoever the man was that had her, he was huge. He dragged her struggling, scantily clad form down three flights out stairs and outside.

It was raining outside, and morbidly, Felicia thought that it was a good thing she was in her bikini.

"LLLLMMMMMPH! ULLLLUMMMPH!" The rain pelted her face, and she struggles became all the more fierce, hoping to catch the attention of someone passing by.

But the street was empty, and all she could do was kick and mumble into this man's hand.

"Mmmmmph! Lllleeellllp!" Looking ahead, she saw that the man was dragging her towards a black car parked at a curb, it's windows tinted.

"Ummmmmph! Mmmmmph!" She kicked and tried to elbow the man, but he didn't react.

One hand still wrapped around her mouth, he used the other to pull open a rear door of the car. Then with ease, he forced the struggling, bikini clad Sheriff inside.

19.

The open palm of Jack's hand connected with Felicia's ass cheek with a loud *TWAP* of skin on skin.

"Nrrrummph!" Felicia groaned into her gag upon feeling the impact.

"We have to stop meeting like this Sheriff, people will start talking."

"Urrrrmmmph!"

Jack came around from behind her and met the eyes of the bound and gagged Sheriff. She held her head up and narrowed her eyes, doing her best to look tough.

"I bet you're thinking of all the things you'd like to do to me right now." He said smugly.

"Grrrrrmmmph!" Her lips pursed around the thick white cloth gagging her as her captor gloated.

"Well let me assure you, I'm thinking of the things I would like to do to you too." He reached a hand around and patted her ass cheek yet again.

"Ulllummmph!" She squealed into her gag and tried to wriggle away as best she could.

After forcing her into the car, the henchman held her there until Jack and his goons came out after a few minutes later. They pulled a thick, white towel tight between her teeth and tied it at the back of her head, and then bound her hands in front of her and bound her feet at the ankles. The car ride seemed to last for ages, and Felicia keep her eyes trained out the window, almost certain that they were going to take her to a deserted spot on the beach to kill her. She was shocked when she saw that they were heading deep into own, in fact, right towards the center of it.

Finally, the car parked in a familiar place and the men roughly carried the bound and gagged Sheriff out in front of Rossi's bar. The main street of town was dead at this time of night, but that didn't stop Felicia from trying to call out for help despite the gag. The men easily forced out the slab of wood that stood where the front window was and forced Felicia inside. Why did they bring her here? Last thing Felicia wanted was for Janet to get mixed up in this more than she already was.

They brought Felicia to the basement, untied her hands and feet, and forced her to hug a slender, metal pillar rising up in a corner. Once she was in place, they tied her hands together again in front of her and around the pillar, and then tied them to the pillar itself about waist high. They then tied her feet together and to the pillar, and Felicia thought that if she could lean down enough then she could pull down her gag, but her hands and feet were tied tight, and she was stuck.

Things only got worse. She had to watch helplessly as the men brought down several large, red containers of gasoline and stack them in a corner. Once the containers were stacked, she watched as they ran long fuses from each to a small device with a timer and wires trailer out of it.

A bomb.

This was it, they were going to blow her up with Rossi's bar.

And now here she was, face to face with Jack. She tugged on her bound hands again but they held tight.

"Oh it's so cute. What happens when you get free? What's your plan? We'll just tie you up again."

"Ummmmph!" She bit the gag in frustration and tugged on her hands again.

"You have spirit Sheriff, I'll give you that."

"Gllllmmmph!" She raised her head to meet his gaze, eyes blazing.

"I'm sure that by now you've figured out what's going to happen. Much like you, Janet Rossi has proven to be stubborn. We offered her a good deal, a great way out, but she refused, and this is what she gets."

"Ullllummmph! Mmmmrrrrgggglle! Lllllummmph!"

"You've presented us with a unique opportunity, we can get rid of both flies in our ointment. Tonight, this place will go up in smoke. The firemen and what passes for a police department will show, and once they get the situation under control they'll find that sweet, little Janet Rossi had our cute little Sheriff tied up in her basement."

"Mmmmmrrrummmph! Ulllmmmph! Mmmmmoooooo!" Felicia resumed her struggles, pulling on the ropes and straining with all her might. If ever that was a time for all those days she spent in the gym for pay off, this would be it.

But the ropes held, and the gag still silenced her.

"Come on poor Sheriff, you're going out as you lived, clad in a barely there bikini."

"Glllllummmph!"

"Poor Janet, she'll go to jail for your kidnapping and death, and Ace will buy the property, and reopen the place. It will still be called Rossi's, you know for tradition and all. There may even be a memorial for you."

"Ummmmph!" She wished that she wasn't gagged just so she could spit in his face.

"Then we gotta retrieve our guns. I gotta call our little mole we have working under you, get them to make a few things happen."

"Ummmph!" She balled her bound fists and leaned forward, glaring at him.

"And you didn't even know that one of your deputies was working for us. I bet it kills you to know?

"Ummmph!"

"Do you want to know who it is? Even if you hadn't fallen into our hands, eventually this person would have betrayed you and handed you over to us. Would you like me to tell you who it is?"

"Ummmm hmmmm! Ummm hmmm!" She nodded, eyes wide.

Maybe if she got out of this then she could use this.

Jack folded his arms and rolled his eyes back.

"Hmmm, no. Sorry, You'll have to go to your grave not knowing."

"Ummmph! Mmmmph!" Felicia pleaded at him through the gag as he turned and walked towards the gasoline and the bomb. Several henchmen were standing by.

"How's it going fellas?"

"All set boss." One replied.

"Great." Jack turned to face Felicia, his finger hovering over the bomb. Her eyes widened and she shook her head.

"Ummm mmmmooo! Mmmmooo!"

"Sorry Sheriff." Jack shrugged and pressed a button on the timer. The digital readout started counting down from "5:00".

"Ummmmph! Mmmmmmph! Glllllmmmmph!" She struggled against her bonds again as Jack strolled forward.

"I am going to miss you, really. You and that sweet little ass." He reached around again and patted her bottom, almost reassuringly.

"Ullllummmph!" Felicia tried to shy away. Jack withdrew his hand and gave her an insulted look.

"Enjoy the countdown." He smiled and turned to head upstairs, followed by his goons.

"Ummmmph! Mmmmmph! Gllllllluuummph!" Felicia mumbled into her gag, watching helplessly as the henchmen filed upstairs one by one until she was alone in the basement with the ticking bomb.

Everything was silent, even the timer, slowly counting until her doom. Felicia gave up on trying to tug on the rope and tried instead to see if she could pull down the pillar.

"Grrrmmmmph! Ullllllmmmph!" She strained and grunted into her gag, first pushing and the switching to pulling.

"Urrrrmmmmph! Lllllrrrrppph!" She strained again and gasped through the gag, it was no use. The pillar was solid concrete. It wasn't budging. This is it, this is how she goes.

3:21 read on the digital timer. She was out of options, almost out of time.

Footsteps echoed from upstairs. Felicia's eyes darted to the ceiling. Yes, someone was walking around up there. It couldn't have been one of Jack's men, they would be long gone by now.

"Ullllummmph! Lllllummmph!" She resumed her struggles.

"Ummmmph! Mmmmmph!" The footsteps got faster and she heard the basement door open.

"Mmmmmph!" Felicia mumbled, her eyes wide. A light came on and someone came approaching from above.

It was Janet, hair back in a ponytail, wearing a tiny pair of black shorts, a black zip up hoodie, and flip flops. She had clearly been sleeping and had left home in a hurry.

"Ummmph! Mmmmph!" Felicia called out to her. Janet hit the bottom of the stairs and stopped, eyes wide, her jaw gaping.

"Felicia?"

"Ummmph!" Felicia nodded.

"What are you doing in my basement? What happened? Why are you tied up? And why are you dressed like that?"

"Ummmph! Mmmmph! Ummmph!" Felicia motioned with her head towards behind Janet, and the bomb, her eyes wide and pleading. Janet turned around and gasped.

"Oh my God, is that..."

"Ummmmph! Mmmmph!" Felicia nodded and tugged at her bonds. Janet had to get her loose and fast or they both would go up.

"Ummm, hang on Felicia." Janet rushed over to the bomb.

"Ummmph! Llllllmmmmph!" Felicia shook her head. *No! What are you doing Janet!*

277

Janet knelt in front of the bomb and turned to face Felicia.

"Hold on, I think I can..." She looked the timer. Just under a minute.

"Gllllrrrmph! Urgggglle!" Felicia pleaded. Now was not the time for Janet to play hero.

But Janet was going to do just that and grabbed a pair of scissors from a nearby shelf.

"Umm, is it the red or blue wire? I've seen this on tv hundreds of times."

"Mmmmmooo! Mmmmmmooo!" Felicia mumbled. If anyone should be disarming this bomb it should be her. It was the blue wire, she knew that from her time in LAPD. Janet turned to face her, eyes wide.

"Was that blue?"

"Mmmmmooo! Mmmmmmooo!" Felicia mumbled.

"Hold on, let me take out that gag." Janet shook her head and stood up.

"Ummmmpph hmmmph! Ummmmpph!" Felicia shook her head. In the time it took for Janet to cross the room, un-gag her, and cross back, the bomb would go off. Janet got the message and froze.

"Blue?" She asked.

"Ummmph!" Felicia nodded, eyes wide.

Janet nodded and turned back to the bomb. She gave Felicia another look and placed the scissors around the blue wire.

"Well, I hope you're right."

"Ummmm..." Felicia nodded. So did she.

Janet squeezed the scissors hard and cut the wire. The digital read out on the timer froze at 0:05.

"Ummmmphhh...." Felicia let out a breath and hung her head. Janet sighed and sat back, also letting out a breath. After a minute, they locked eyes.

"I take it there's a story here." Janet said

"Ummm hmmm..." Felicia nodded.

"I'll untie you and you can tell me." Janet got up and approached the still bound Sheriff.

20.

Felicia took a long sip from the glass of beer Janet served her and set

it down on the table. Across from her, Janet was nursing a glass of

wine. She had offered Felicia some but Felicia was always a beer

girl, and Janet happened to keep a small stock of beer around her

apartment in "the rare case I have company" she said as she poured

Felicia her glass.

Janet's apartment was nice, not too big or small, and neatly kept and

organized. They both sat at a small dining room table big enough for

two which was located next to Janet's living room, which was

occupied by a flat screen, a couch, and several shelves of DVD's.

After disarming the bomb, Janet quickly untied Felicia and they both

hurried up and out of the basement. Of course Janet suggested

calling the police but Felicia insisted against it, saying she would explain later. But Felicia was also worried that Jack and his men would return and notice that their plan had not played out as they hoped, so they smashed the detonator. The bar basement had a drain in the middle, so they also dumped out the drums of gas. After leaving, they replaced the wooden slab, rather haphazardly, in front of the broken door and hurried home, weary and smelling of gasoline.

Felicia felt awkward riding home with Janet because she was still clad in only the tiny bikini, and from the driver's seat she noticed Janet sneaking looks her way. Once they got to Janet's place, only a few minutes from the bar, she gave Felicia a robe to wear.

"I don't know about you, but I could use a drink." Janet said as she headed towards her kitchen. Felicia couldn't agree more. So Janet poured Felicia her beer and herself a glass of wine and they sat and Felicia told her tale. Once she finished, Janet took a long sip from her wine.

"Your first mistake was trusting Shelly Arnold." She said rolling her eyes.

"Why is that?" Felicia asked. Of all the parties to blame for this, all Shelly did was push her in the right direction.

Or did she? Was it a set up? No, how could Shelly know that she would get caught, she would be gambling with a lot of factors that she had no control over.

"Shelly's as dirty and as crooked as they get. Her husband...ex husband...was in the drug business, not big but not small time either. He decided to try and take on Ace for control of this town."

Felicia's eyes widened.

"Did Ace kill him?"

Janet shook her head.

"No, her husband was stupid, got caught by the FBI and went away for a long time. Shelly left him and took most of his money with her. Now she has plans to start her own operation and finish what her husband started."

Felicia swallowed hard and took a long, long gulp from her beer. Fuck, she had allowed herself to be played.

"So, she sent me to that place hoping that I would bust them, take in Ace's top man. Eliminate the competition for her."

Janet nodded.

"Or she figured that eventually you would go after her, eliminate you before you become a threat. Either situation would be a win for her."

That would explain those photos Shelly had of Tanya too, hell she probably took them herself! Dammit, this town!

She gritted her teeth and wrapped her hand around her glass. Janet's eyes widened and she leaned forward and placed her hand on Felicia's. Her touch sent a static charge through Felicia, a shiver ran up her spine and she felt her body break out in gooseflesh. A gasp escaped Felicia's lips, Janet's skin was soft, delicate, and her nails raked so gently against Felicia. There was something about Janet, a quiet energy, she probably drove men crazy in this town.

"It's okay," Janet reassured her. " How could you know?"

Felicia locked eyes with Janet, those brown eyes staring at her from under the glasses.

"It's my job to know. I promised to protect this town, to protect you."

Janet withdrew her hand.

"Do you yourself a favor and leave while you can. This place has a habit of chaining someone down."

Janet went to take another sip of wine and noticed her glass was empty. She got up and stalked back to the kitchen, and Felicia used that opportunity to get up and walk off some frustration. Felicia made her way into the living room and noticed that there wasn't much in the way of decorations, or even pictures.

"You said you don't get company often?" Felicia asked

"Not really, every now and then a family member will come visit." Janet answered and Felicia heard the refrigerator door open.

"No boyfriend?"

"In this town? Hell no. That doesn't stop them from trying though." Janet replied, and Felicia couldn't repress her smile. That confirmed what she thought, that Janet had men lining up, but she had interest in what they had to offer.

Felicia was about to head back to the table when she noticed a small table, about waist high, set against a wall. The only thing on the table was a black, plain book. Felicia found herself drifting towards it, intrigued. So maybe Janet did have a sentimental side after all? As she got closer, she saw that the book was a photo album, the edges of the laminated paper sticking out gave it away. Her fingers gripped the edge of the cover and she flipped it to the first page.

Felicia's jaw dropped. It was not what she expected.

Mounted on the first page of the album was a picture of Janet, but a very different Janet. She had to be at least ten years younger, her mouth spread in a wide grin displaying dazzling white teeth, wearing a pink bikini and was laying on her side on a sandy beach, the sun setting dazzlingly behind her. It wasn't how Janet looked, or even how sexy she was in that bikini, it was that this just wasn't some pic someone took at a beach. Janet's hair and make-up were perfect, flawless, and the lighting was just... well perfect. This was a professional photo.

Janet used to be a model?

Felicia couldn't help but gawk at it. She could tell that Janet had great breasts, but this bikini just proved that, and her abs were a tight and solid. Flipping to the next page, she saw that it was filled with photos of Janet in various lingerie and bikinis. Janet was stunning, absolutely stunning. In one photo, she was topless, her hands over her large breasts, and half turned to the camera, showing off her ass in a white thong bikini bottom. Her glutes were tan and tight, and the thong disappeared into her rear and showed off her goods perfectly.

Felicia was about to flip the page when a hand shot out and slammed the book shut. She jumped back and found herself staring in Janet's fiery eyes.

"What are you doing?" Janet demanded, glaring at her.

"I'm sorry, it was jus-"

"Why were you looking through this?" She held the book up in front of Felicia's face.

"I..." Felicia stammered. "I just wanted to know... was just curious."

Janet slammed the book down on the table.

"Well, don't go snooping through my stuff!"

"Janet I'm sorry, I-you.. you were a model?"

Janet sighed and set the book back on the table.

"I was. Not anymore." She turned away.

"Janet those pictures," Felicia followed after her. "I used to be in the industry, those were great. You were-"

"What?" Janet spun around to face her. "What was I? Beautiful?"

"You still are." Felicia said.

Janet stammered, taken aback by the comment. Felicia wasn't lying, Janet was still gorgeous. Age had been very kind to her.

"I... I'm sorry I snapped. I don't like to talk about it."

Felicia reached out an arm and rubbed Janet's shoulder.

"It's okay. Janet, I... I owe you my life. I don't know how I can ever repay you. You can tell me."

Their eyes met. For the first time, Felicia could see that Janet had softened, let her guard down just a bit. Her eyes were wide, wounded, wary.

"I spent some time in LA, got swept up in "The biz" as they call it. Everyone said I was due for great things."

"But?"

"But, my dad got sick, I packed up and moved back to help, and here I am." Janet motioned to the apartment around them. "This place, it chains you down. I don't want to see you chained down with me."

Janet turned away and headed for a darkened room. She reached in and flipped a switch, revealing a large bathroom. Felicia could see a tub with a sliding glass door set against the side wall.

"Anyway, I still smell like gas, I think I'm gonna have a shower. You could probably use one too." She gave Felicia a look and stepped in the bathroom, but didn't close the door.

From the hallway, Felicia watched as Janet reached into the shower and turned on the water. She ran her hand under the screaming water, testing the temperature, all the while acting like she was oblivious to Felicia's presence. Finally satisfied with the water, Janet stepped back from the shower and kicked off her flip flops.

Then she pulled the tie out of her hair and shook her brown locks free. With her back still to Felicia, Janet unzipped the hoodie. She shrugged the baggy garment down, first exposing her bare shoulders, brown with the exception of tan lines that ran along her shoulder blades and along the back of her neck. The hoodie dropped to the floor, and Janet wore nothing underneath. Then, she gripped the sides of her shorts and started to slide them down her hips. The garment came down slowly, first exposing the top of a pair of black thong panties. Her shorts slid down along the curve of her ass, slowly revealing her well tanned, toned tush to Felicia. Janet's ass hadn't changed at all from those pictures.

Felicia realized her heart was pounding and she didn't bother to suppress the gasp that escaped her lips. The shorts slid down along Janet's legs and landed in a heap on the floor. Janet lazily kicked the shorts aside and gripped either side of the panties, and Felicia felt her heart kick into overdrive. Before she knew it, her hands were caressing her own thighs and she felt the skin rise.

Back in the bathroom, Janet slid down the panties, exposing a tan line that matched perfectly. The panties slid down Janet's legs and to the floor with ease. Now completely nude, but still never turning around, Janet stepped into the shower and slid the door shut behind her. Felicia's hands glided from her outer thigh to her inner thigh, up her leg...

Inside the bathroom, the glass shower door fogged up. Felicia could still see a blurry outline of Janet inside. Janet reached for something from a shelf above her, and Felicia saw Janet's breasts bounce as she moved. Meanwhile, Felicia's hands drifted to her crotch, and she could feel the moisture down there.

Before she could second guess herself, she untied the robe and let it slide off her shoulders. She still wore the bikini underneath. She strode forward into the bathroom and closed the door behind her. Steam quickly started filling the room. Then she was across the room and gripping the handle of the shower door. It slid open easily, and Janet spun around, wet hair clinging to her shoulders, water flowing along her wet breasts. Janet's nipples stood erect as she eyed Felicia. Felicia stepped inside and slid the door shut behind her.

Their lips met, locking onto each other. Janet grabbed a handful of Felicia's hair and pulled her forward under the cascading water as they kissed. Felicia's hands ran along Janet's breasts, wishing they could become one with the water and flow over Janet's entire body. They kissed some more and Felicia slid her tongue into Janet's mouth. Their tongues met and danced over each other. Felicia was soaked now.

Janet's hand slid to the back of Felicia's neck and undid the knot holding up the bikini top while her other hand slid to Felicia's shoulder working on the other knot. Felicia pulled Janet close and slid her hands along Janet's bare back to her ass. Much like the rest of her, Janet's ass was soft, and Felicia's fingers ran down either cheek, tightening, squeezing. She wanted it, wanted it all.

Janet pulled off Felicia's top and pulled her close, their breasts touching, mashing into each others. They kissed again, deeply.

Janet slid her face down Felicia's neck, to her chest, then her breasts. Felicia let out a sigh as Janet's tongue flicked over her nipples. Ecstasy ran through her breasts and Janet's tongue danced over them, lapping up the water that ran over them. Felicia reached out to run her hands through Janet's hair but Janet caught them and pushed them together, giving Felicia a "tsk tsk" look as she did. Then she spun Felicia around and pushed her towards the front of the shower, raising her hands above her as she did.

Felicia's hands bumped against the shower head and Janet held them there with one hand while raising Felicia's bikini top up with another. In seconds, Janet had wrapped the top around Felicia's hands, securing them to the shower head. After securing Felicia's hands, Janet planted another deep kiss on her as the water cascaded over them.

Felicia gave in, leaning her head back and letting Janet kiss her deeply. Janet withdrew and slid her tongue down Felicia's neck, between her breasts, along her abs, her navel, and stopping just as her bikini bottoms.

Felicia sighed as Janet's fingers glided along her hips, tracing the side of the bottoms. Her fingers continued along Felicia's ass cheeks, sliding down them and back up as Felicia moaned in pleasure. Janet grabbed the back of the bikini bottoms and slid them off with ease. Another moan escaped Felicia's lips as Janet's tongue worked along her thigh, and up-

-Up over her navel, her abs, to her breasts... Janet was rising, bikini bottoms still in hand.

"Being a little too noisy." Janet giggled.

"I'm sorry, I just..." Another moan.

Janet grabbed a small, white wash cloth and placed it into Felicia's mouth. Felicia looked at her with pleading eyes.

"This won't take long, I like to work in silence."

"Ummm-Hmmmm..." Felicia moaned into her gag.

Janet then slid the g-string bikini bottom over Felicia's head, the bottom of it snapping into place over the gag in her mouth. Felicia regarded Janet with wide eyes.

"Ummmmmm..." Felicia moaned. Janet giggled and leaned forward, biting on the g-string, her hands rubbing on Felicia's breasts. She kissed Felicia's gagged mouth, one hand rubbing her breast while the other slid down Felicia's torso.

"Ugggghhhh---mmmmmmph!" The gag muffled Felicia's moan of pleasure.

Janet bit into the gag, her eyes meeting Felicia's.

Felicia felt Janet's hand slide along her smooth crotch, and down...

She felt a tingle of pleasure as Janet's finger found her spot. Her entire body convulsed.

Janet let go of the gag and stooped down, running her tongue along Felicia's nipples.

"Grrrmmmmm" Felicia moaned.

Meanwhile, Janet's finger danced across her vagina, stroking her, flicking her, pushing. More convulsing. Janet's head slid down lower.

"Mmmmmmph! Mmmmpph!" Felicia tried to contain herself but she couldn't. Her entire body rocked with Janet's touches.

Then she felt Janet's finger slid inside her.

"Ummmmph! Mmmmmmph! Glllllllmmmm" Felicia moaned.

Janet's tongue ran along Felicia's crotch, between her lips, and up-

"Mmmmmmmph!"

There it was, Janet's tongue played over her clit while her finger danced inside Felicia. Her entire body shook, her bound hands tightened into fists. She could feel the damn welling up, getting ready to burst...

"Ummmmppph! Mmmmmph!" Another set of convulsions rocked her. She bit into her gag with all her might.

"Glllllummph!" Janet sucked on her clit.

Felicia's entire body shook and she came.

"Hmmmmmmmph! Ummmmmph! Mmmmmmphh!"

21.

Janet groaned as the harsh morning sun shown in through the thin, white drapes of her bedroom window. It was time time for another day at the bar.

If the bar was even still standing.

Her eyes drifted open and the events of the previous night came flooding back: The alarm going off at the bar, showing up there to find Felicia, bound and gagged in her micro-bikini in the basement, the bomb, and then the shower.

The shower. They made love two more times after that. Felicia seemed willing to let Janet take the lead. Janet found that she always had a dominant personality in the bedroom, and Felicia seemed to accept that. Later, as they drifted off to sleep, Janet realized that maybe gagging Felicia wasn't the wisest course of action given what had happened earlier in the night, but Felicia didn't seem to mind.

Janet sat up, holding the blanket over her bare chest, and looked down at Felicia's naked, sleeping body. She was out, resting peacefully, and Janet decided that it would be for the best to let her sleep. From what Janet understood, Felicia had a mole in her organization, and had to face her men today with that knowledge.

Poor girl, signed up for this with no idea of what she was in for. Janet ran a hand through Felicia's hair. She had been through so much already, and was bound for much more trouble if she continued. Part of Janet admired Felicia for being so adamant about pursuing Justice, but the rest of her was scared. Felicia was a good girl, a great girl, and Janet didn't want her getting hurt. They could both leave this place together, Janet could sell the bar to Ace, and they could go anywhere.

But she knew that Felicia would never, that she would fight for Janet's bar. It was comforting in a way, to have someone in this town looking out for her, she had never had that before.

Janet gave Felicia's hair another stroke and got up. Part of her considered not even opening the bar today, but she had to, had to show that she wasn't scared, and wasn't giving up.

But they'll just come again, and it will be worse. Somehow. She would just have to take that, somehow, and hope Felicia didn't get mixed in somehow.

She let the covers fall and stepped out of the bed, completely nude, and looked down at her sleeping lover. Felicia lay on her stomach, and the covers were pushed halfway down her excellent ass, exposing quite a bit of her crack. Janet considered pulling them up, but decided to enjoy the sight a bit.

Janet made her way over to her dresser and pulled out a pair of thong panties, white with pink trim around the top. She slipped them on and then added a matching bra, followed by black tights. She completed the outfit with a white beater and a white button down shirt. The top few buttons of the shirt were left open, revealing plenty of her cleavage, then she pulled her hair back into a ponytail and put on her glasses. Before heading out, she turned to admire Felicia's sleeping form again. It was wishful thinking to hope that Felicia would be waiting here when she got back, but the thought comforted her. It had been years since she had a night of passion like last night, and she very much wanted another one. Somehow, she knew though that even if Felicia didn't wait up for her, that somehow they would find a way into each other's arms again tonight.

Janet allowed herself a small smile and then headed out of the bedroom.

Somewhat to her surprise, the bar was still standing when she got there. She opened quickly and considered hammering the wooden board back over the shattered door, but who was she kidding, it hadn't deterred Ace's goons from breaking and entering before. The morning went smooth but slowly, and it felt strange to her to continue to operate as if nothing was wrong, as if someone hadn't tried to burn this place to the ground with Felicia in it, hoping to pin it all on her. That may have been what infuriated Janet the most, that they wanted to set her up for the death of the Sheriff, and spitefully she hoped that Felicia did nail these guys, but she knew that was wishful thinking.

So she acted like it was any other day, cleaning the bar and tables, preparing the kitchen. Her cook, Alex, didn't come in until 3 for the dinner rush, and she liked to leave his work space neat and tidy.

Next she placed a call to a window company to replace the shattered window, though she suspected it would prove a futile gesture.

At around noon she got her first patrons, two women. One was a shorter but stunning Latina with dark skin, darker hair, and a great body. Her breast looked to be about a C-Cup but she wore a leopard print crop top and had her breasts pushed up to give everyone a nice view. She also wore short black shorts that accentuated her real asset: her behind. The Latina's ass protruded nicely, but round and firm, it could give Felicia's a good run for it's money.

Her companion was a dark haired white girl, maybe late 20's. This girl was very clearly a bodybuilder, her black crop top showing off her toned, feminine muscles. She wasn't one of those female bodybuilders that looked masculine, in fact her physique gave her a stature like that of a female superhero. Her breasts were large and obviously enhanced, and she had the butt of a woman who knew the right amount of squats to do to keep it tight.

Janet didn't recognize either of them and took them for tourists. They sat at the bar and ordered waters. She served them and they sat and enjoyed their drinks wordlessly.

"You two waiting for someone?" Janet asked, trying to play good bartender and make conversation.

The Latina nodded while the bodybuilder only sipped.

"Want drink menus? We don't start serving food until 3."

The Latina shook her head. Warning bells started going off in Janet's head. Something was seriously off about all this. Could they be with Ace? She knew that he dealt in girls but he typically didn't use them as muscle.

Or maybe the Latina didn't speak English, but then what about her friend? Janet shook her head, all of this stuff was making her paranoid. These two could just be dumb, stuck up tourists for all she knew.

"Don't talk much do you?"

"Does the Sheriff come by here?" The Bodybuilder asked. "The hot one, I mean. The one in the papers."

"She does tend to stop by, yes. Do you need to talk to her."

The Latina nodded. Janet sighed.

"I can give you directions to the police station, you'll find her there."

"What about here? She like, hangs out here?" The Bodybuilder asked.

"If you say so."

"Could you call her? Ask her to stop by."

What the hell? Why did they want the Sheriff? If it was something serious then they could go to the station.

"Is something wrong? Did something happen to you two?" She asked, hoping to give them the benefit of the doubt.

"We're waiting for a friend, she wants to meet the Sheriff. They used to know each other." The Bodybuilder explained as the Latina nodded along.

"Look, I don't know if she'll be here. If you want to talk to her, go to the station." Janet stepped away from the bar and grabbed a white towel, deciding to remove herself from what ever was going on here.

She stepped out from behind the bar, noticing that both women never took their eyes off of her. Could they be friends of Felicia's from her modeling days? They mentioned the papers, maybe they saw the photo and came to see if she was alright.

As Janet made her way towards a booth to wipe it off, both women got off of their stools and approached her. She froze as the Latina took up a position behind her and the Bodybuilder loomed in front of her. Janet eyed her up, there was no way she could overpower this woman.

"Look, could you just like, get ahold of her, ask her to come here. Say it's a surprise."

Janet glared at her, she could feel her blood pumping, her heart pounding. This was getting bad.

"Get out of my bar."

"Or what," The Bodybuilder smiled. "You'll call the Sheriff?"

Janet balled her fists. If she ran, she would crash right into the Latina, and she didn't want to call Felicia and get her mixed up in more trouble. Her eyes wandered over to the bar, she stood right next to it, if she was fast then she could jump over it and make her way out the back door. Then what? Call Felicia? These two would attempt to follow, no doubt, she would have to lose them.

"I'm going to ask you one more time, leave." She looked the Bodybuilder square in the eye, trying to mask her fear.

"Well, we won't. Guess you'll have to call the Sheriff." She said in a mocking tone.

Janet gritted her teeth and knew she had only one option.

She threw the towel in the bodybuilder's face and lunged for the bar. Behind her, the Latina dived after her, arms outstretched. Janet gripped the edges of the bar and started to pull herself over when she felt the Latina's hands dig into the waist band of her pants and pull. Her fingers wrapped around the edge of the bar she pitched herself forward and over it. As she lunged over the bar, she felt her pants slip down, exposing her ass as the Latina pulled.

Fuck it! She thought and heaved herself forward.

The Latina continued to pull as Janet scrambled over the edge of the bar and she felt her tights slip down past her ass to her legs. She kicked as she tumbled forward and felt the Latina let go. Janet pitched forward headfirst to the other side of the bar, landing in a heap on the other side. Feet pounded on the other side of the bar and she knew that the two women were running around to get her.

Janet pushed herself up and turned to run, not noticing that her black tights were bunched up around her ankles. She felt her feet get wrapped up in her pants and she pitched forward, holding her hands out to pad her fall. Her palms smacked against the hard ground as she hit.

Shit!

She rolled over and gripped her pants, hoping to pull them up enough for her to easily run.

Too late. Both women were on her side and converged on her. Janet spun around to crawl away, but the Bodybuilder grabbed her by either arm and pulled her up.

"Hey, get off of me! Hey!" She tried to kick her legs, still tangled up in her pants.

The Latina came around to her front and eyed her, smiling.

"What are you doing? Let go of me!" Janet continued to struggle.

A grin spread from ear to ear on the Latina and she leaned forward, gripped the shoulders of Janet's top, and pulled them down. The shirt came down, but the buttons still held, the top half of her shirt flipping down as the Latina pushed, pinning her arms to her side.

"Hey! What the hell!" Janet struggled, realized that the Latina pushed down Janet's beater as well, exposing her bra. The Latina's eyes were on fire as she stared at Janet's breasts as she struggled.

"What the-" She tried to raise her arms but her shirt kept them pinned down against her now bare legs.

"Help! Help! H-uuuuuummmmph!" Her cry was cut up by the thick white towel being thrown over her head and pulled back between her teeth by the Bodybuilder.

"Ummmmph! Mmmmmmmph!" Janet bit down on the gag as she felt it being knotted at the back of her head.

"Glllmmmph! Mlllllrrrgglle!" Janet struggled, gagged and exposed. She looked down to see the Latina squatting down, caressing her bare leg as she went.

"Ummmph!" Janet kicked at her. The Latina only smiled and grabbed the tights bunched around Janet's feet. In a minute, the Latina had wrapped them in a knot around her feet, tying Janet's legs together.

"Ulllluggggle! Ummmmph!" Janet struggled as the Latina wrapped her hands around her feet.

"Let's get her out of sight." The Bodybuilder said behind her. They picked Janet's struggling form up, the Bodybuilder holding Janet by the arms, and carried her towards the kitchen.

"Mmmmph! Ummmmph! Gllmmmmph!" Janet mumbled into her gag as they carried her.

They kicked open the swinging kitchen doors and set her down on the floor in front of the oven.

"Mmmmph! Ummmph!" Janet tried to raise her arms again with no luck.

Both women stood over her. Janet met their eyes and glared.

"Just hang here alright, maybe if you're a good girl we'll come back and let you go once this is all over."

"Mmmmmuuummph mmmmmooo!" Janet mouthed into the gag.

"No need to be rude about this, it's not you we want. Play along and you'll be fine."

"Ummmph!" Janet mumbled, but then met their eyes. There was sincerity in the Bodybuilders face, in fact, she looked almost sad. As for the Latina, her wide eyes ran over Janet's bound form with lust.

"Just..." The Bodybuilder searched for the right words, "Hang tight."

"Glllummunngh" Janet rolled her eyes.

Both women turned to leave, though the Latina kept stealing looks back at Janet. In fact, the Bodybuilder had to grab her by the shoulder and pull her out. Then she was alone, tied up in her own kitchen.

Now what? They said they would let her go, but could she trust them? Her cook came in at 3, so maybe she could hold out until then?

"Mmmm..." she wriggled, trying to get comfortable. The floor was cold on her bare ass cheeks. No, she couldn't wait, she had to find a way out. Whoever these two were, they wanted Felicia. They mentioned someone else, someone that wanted to meet Felicia. Were they going to use Janet as bait to bring Felicia to this person. If it wasn't Ace, then who? Janet had a feeling that things were about to

get ugly. She tugged on her hands, trying to loosen the shirt wrapped

around her waist, but it held tight, keeping them pinned. In fact, it

felt like they had actually knotted her sleeves together as well.

Shit, now what? She always considered herself a Dom, sexually, and

was used to gagging other women, but this was the first time she had

ever been gagged.

Her eyes raced around the kitchen. Where were the knives? She

realized that she rarely spent time in here, mostly letting her cook do

his thing. If she got out of this, that would have to change.

There! Organized by size in a knife block were several kitchen

knives. The knife block sat in the corner of a shelf on the other side

of the kitchen. She would have to wriggle, or hop, over and cut

herself free. Then it was just a matter of taking out her gag and pulling her pants up. It did dawn on her that she was literally caught with her pants down. If not for the gag then Janet would have cracked a smile.

"Grrrmmmm" She grunted into the gag and used her feet to pull herself forward. Her bare ass slid along the cool ground, causing an involuntary "Mhmmmm!" of annoyance from her. This couldn't go on, she would have to try standing.

Janet slid back, pressing herself flat against a cabinet and placed her palms flat against it.

"Urrrrmmm! Mrrrrrmmmm!" She grunted and bit into that gag as she used her bound feet to push herself up, steadying herself with her hands. Eventually her hands found the edge of the countertop and she gripped it and pushed herself into a standing position, allowing herself a muffled sigh of relief.

So much for small victories, now to get to the knife. Janet stood as straight as she could and hopped forward. She could feel her breasts bounce and heave as she moved and she rolled her eyes. Another hop. Step by step she was growing closer to the knives.

Another hop and she felt herself wobble and pitch forward.

"Hhhmmmm..." She started into her gag and stopped, now wanting to draw attention. Her hands pinwheeled at her sides and she pressed her feet flat to the ground, trying with all her might not to fall on her face. Janet teetered backwards and arched her back straight, pressing her hands flat to her side. The world stopped spinning and she found her balance again. And the knives were closer. Another small hop brought her to the island in the center of the kitchen.

Janet leaned back against the island, allowing herself a minute to breath and collect herself. Halfway there, she was halfway there. She can't afford to fuck up now, just make it to the knives and cut the shirt free, that's all. After that, she would escape through the back door, find Felicia and warn her about these crazy bitches after her. Felicia had a knack for getting into trouble alright, she'll give her that.

She gritted her teeth around her gag and stood up, facing the knives, ready to cut her way to freedom.

"Ay!" a voice called out behind her.

"Ummmmph!" Janet starting hopping like bunny on steroids, her feet stamping on the ground as she made her way to the knives. Behind her, she heard frenzied footsteps rushing towards her, and something that was probably cursing in Spanish.

They were only a few feet away! Janet kept hopping-

-Hands seized her from behind and pulled her back. A high pitched voice chattered away in her ear in Spanish.

"Uuummmhhmmm! Mrrrrggggle!" Janet kicked and tried to elbow her captor, but the Latina hooked her arms through Janet's and dragged her back.

"Mrrrrmmmpummmphh! Grrrlllummbbbbhh!" Janet shook her head and mumbled into her gag in rage and frustration.

The doors burst open and the Bodybuilder rushed in.

"What's going on?" She asked.

The Latina answered in Spanish, going a mile a minute while twisting Janet around to face the Bodybuilder.

"Whoa, whoa!" The Bodybuilder held up a hand. "Slow down, in English!"

"Tight ass here was trying to get a blade!" the Latina remarked in a heavy accent.

"You really think she has a tight ass?" the Bodybuilder looked hurt and ran her hands along her own shapely behind.

"Si!" The Latina smacked Janet's behind.

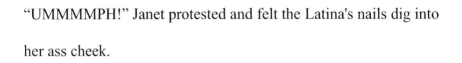

"UMMMMPH!" Janet protested and felt the Latina's nails dig into her ass cheek.

"Fine, set her down." The Bodybuilder stalked across the kitchen, but her eyes kept straying to Janet's thonged ass.

Keep staring, honey. Janet thought, glaring at the Bodybuilder as the Latina set her against a wall. On the other side of the room, the Bodybuilder picked up the knife block.

"I mean, not tighter than my ass, right?" She asked.

The Latina squatted down in front of Janet and rolled her eyes, and muttered a few words in Spanish. Then her eyes met Janet's. There was no mistaking it, the Latina's eyes were filled with lust.

"Ummm?" Janet asked through the gag.

The Latina responded by running one of her perfectly manicured nails along Janet's cheek and smiling, showing brilliant, white teeth.

"Murrggllle..." Janet recoiled as the Latina ran her finger over the gag, down along Janet's neck to her chest, and finally, along her breast.

"Muuuurrrmmph!" Janet stamped her feet as the Latina's finger danced along the top of her breast. She lowered her head to see the woman's finger stroking down, towards the edge of her bra-

"Hey!" the Bodybuilder came up behind the Latina, arms crossed. The Latina rolled her eyes and stood up. Janet breathed a sigh of relief.

"Why do you have to be so weird?" The Bodybuilder demanded, to which the Latina shrugged. Block of knives still in hand, the Bodybuilder looked down at Janet.

"Come on, let's go." She grabbed the Latina by the arm and lead her towards the kitchen door, but the Latina's eyes stayed on Janet. The two woman exited, leaving Janet alone, but she could still feeling the lingering effects of the Latina's touch and realized that she would have to make a point to never be left alone with that woman.

Her eyes raced around the kitchen again for a way of escape. Maybe she could try to use the oven burners to burn through her shirt? It would be a risky move, and could end with her or the bar catching on fire. Another idea was that she could just try to hop out the back door and find someone free her, but she shook her head and banished the thought. There was no way she would allow herself to be seen in public, half naked, bound with her own clothes and gagged. She would find a way out of here, somehow.

Janet leaned her head back and closed her eyes, thinking. Her captors would be on guard after her latest attempt, so she had to make them lower their guard, to think that she was a nice, helpless, docile damsel. If they found drawing attention or trying to escape again they may knock her out or lock her in a closet, or worse. She figured that if she gave it a few minutes then they would relax and she could squirm her way around the kitchen and see what she could use to get free and hopefully warn Felicia.

The sound of voices brought her back to reality. Two women were talking out in the bar. She strained to hear. She couldn't detect any accent in either voice, so it wasn't the Latina. Another minute of listening and she could pick out the Bodybuilder's voice, but the other? Janet held her breath and listened

Then her eyes widened when she realized she did recognize the second voice. Felicia! Shit!

Janet leaned forward, hoping that she could see out of the window set in the double kitchen doors, but she was too far. The voices continued. She scooted forward. Both women sounds cordial, relaxed.

"Mmmmph! Ummmmph!" She mumbled, hoping Felicia could hear her muffled cries.

But the voices continued in normal, conversational tone.

"Gllllummmph!"

Shit! Now what? Felicia was going to fall right into their trap. Her mind raced, and she realized what her only option was, her last, desperate option. She looked at the double doors, the window looking out into the bar, and realized what she had to do.

With no other choice, Janet bit into her gag and started to push herself up.

22.

Felicia woke up with the blankets half off, naked and alone in Janet's bed. The harsh morning sun spilled in through the bedroom window, breaking Felicia out of a deep, dreamless sleep. She stretched, rolled over, and reached a hand out to the other side of the bed, hoping to find Janet's soft skin, to stroke her bare breast. Instead, all she found was mattress, and rolled over to find the other side of the bed empty. She wasn't shocked though, in fact, she found herself oddly at peace with it.

She went over the events of the previous night in her head, still not believing parts of it had happened. Maybe their hormones were up because they both were almost blown up, or at least that's what she told herself. They had both given each other multiple orgasms, and Janet was, well, a goddess. Janet clearly was experienced, and very aggressive. Felicia almost objected to Janet gagging her in the shower, giving the events of the past few days, but in the end she let Janet have her way. There was something oddly relaxing about being helpless and at Janet's mercy, and something very sexual about it all.

But what to do now? She guessed that Janet had gone to the bar, which took guts after last night, but Janet seemed like the type that wouldn't back down until the very end. Felicia admired her for that, especially since she realized that she didn't even want to get out of bed, let alone go into the station today. Maybe she would just wait here, naked in bed, for Janet to return, and make love again. Janet would gag her again, and Felicia trusted Janet enough that she would let her gag her as much as she wanted.

Felicia stroked her bare nipple at the thought and felt herself getting wet. Yes, it sounded beautiful, but she knew that she would have to go out. The remains of the bomb were still at the bar and needed to be taken in for evidence, not to mention that she now had to find out who on her force was working for Ace. She wanted to put 24 hour surveillance on Janet's bar, but she couldn't trust any of her troopers to do it. In fact, she couldn't trust anyone now. The thought sobered her and she lifted her finger away from her erect nipple.

She could just leave with Janet, go back to L.A, get on the force again there.

No, she promised Janet she would save her bar. She had promised this town she would save it. If she left then Ace won. Felicia also knew that most of the town didn't take her serious, that they thought she was just a pretty face playing cops and robbers, and if she left she would prove those people right too.

Felicia would stay, she would find the mole, and take Ace down. She sat up and decided to get dressed, but then realized that the only clothes she had were the skimpy bikini and the robe Janet had let her borrow.

She retrieved the still wet micro bikini from the shower and slipped it on, then threw her robe over it before realizing she had no car, since her vehicle was presumably still back at the apartment building where she was caught. Did Marston's Pointe have a cab service? Though that didn't matter either, she had no money for a cab. An idea crossed her mind to call the station and ask for a pickup, but she didn't want any of her men to pick her up dressed like this.

In the end, she stripped out of the bikini and hung it over Janet's shower to dry. Part of her considered throwing it away, but in a strange way she liked it. It was as exposing as a bikini could get, but it made her feel sexy, especially after what happened between her and Janet last night. She raided Janet's closet and found a small pair of spandex workout shorts. The shorts were tight, skin tight, and she found that she had to keep picking at them to keep them from riding up and exposing her ass cheeks. Next she found a black tank top and slipped it on. The top was a little big, given that Janet's breasts are much larger, so Felicia finished with a black hoodie that fit snugly. She finished it off with the pair of flip-flops she had see Janet wearing the previous night. Now, it was time to walk home.

The day was warm and beautiful, and she took in a breath of fresh

air as she exited Janet's apartment building. She didn't know how far

of a walk it would be to her place but she didn't care, wanting to

delay her arrival at the police station as much as she could. In fact,

she didn't want to go in at all, and wasn't she entitled to a day off,

especially given recent events? As she thought about this, she could

feel the too small shorts start to crunch up in her ass crack and

stopped to pick it, not knowing what was more embarrassing:

constantly picking at the shorts or allowing her ass cheeks to be

exposed to the whole town?

She walked some more and realized she recognized the part of town

she was in. It was the main street, the main business area, Janet's bar

was right in this stretch! Would it be too forward to stop in a visit?

The practical side of her told her to keep walking, stop at home,

change, and call for a patrol car to get her, but she also didn't want to

face her fellow officers. One drink at Janet's wouldn't hurt, right?

Just one drink, a little chit-chat, she would apologize for borrowing clothes, offer to return them that night, and be off. As she turned a corner, she saw the bar and made a decision. Yes, she would stop in for one drink, maybe check out the bomb, just to be official, and leave.

She entered the bar with a smile on her face, but then found herself taken off guard when she saw that Janet wasn't behind the bar, but a short, muscular dark haired woman. The muscle didn't take away from the woman's beauty, in fact, they accented her femininity nicely. As Felicia walked in she caught the woman look up at her with a start as she stashed something that looked like a knife block under the bar.

Movement caught Felicia's eye and she saw a dark skinned Latino woman stepping out from behind the bar, her eyes widen and on Felicia as well.

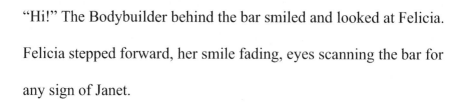

"Hi!" The Bodybuilder behind the bar smiled and looked at Felicia. Felicia stepped forward, her smile fading, eyes scanning the bar for any sign of Janet.

"Is Janet around?" She asked.

The Bodybuilder exchanged a look with the Latina, who was taking a seat at the far end of the bar.

"She's tied up in something right now," The Bodybuilder said. "Could I get you a drink?"

"I didn't know Janet had help around here." Felicia said, stepping forward. She supposed it made sense, Janet couldn't do it all by herself.

"We're new hires, new in town actually. Say, aren't you the new Sheriff around here?" The Bodybuilder asked.

"I'm off duty." Felicia nodded, feeling the shorts bunching again. She picked them out of her ass as she stepped towards the bar.

"Well, want a drink?" The Bodybuilder asked again.

"Is she here?" Felicia asked.

"What?" The Bodybuilder's eyes went wide.

"Janet? Is she here?" Felicia took a seat opposite the Bodybuilder.

"Oh," The other woman laughed. "Sorry, she had to run out for a bit. Should be right back, want a drink while you wait?"

"No, I... I just want to talk with her. Official business."

"Sure." The Bodybuilder nodded.

"She didn't say anything to you, did she?"

"She hasn't done much talking today." The Bodybuilder smiled.

"Not about the basement or anything?"

"Nope." The Bodybuilder shook her head.

Felicia nodded.

"I guess I can wait for a bit then." She settled in her chair.

"Want something to drink to pass the time?" The girl asked, and Felicia gave her a look. This was one pushy bartender.

"I just... it's been a slow day, you know? I want to feel useful." She gave Felicia an awkward smile.

"Sure, I'll have beer." Felicia nodded, and turned towards the Latina, who sat on the other side of the bar, watching Felicia.

"What's your story?"

"Oh, Eva there is our new waitress. Doesn't speak English well."
The Bodybuilder said, her back to Felicia.

"And you are?" Felicia turned back to look at the Bodybuilder. Her back was still to Felicia, and she could see the muscles in her back and shoulders work as she moved. The Bodybuilder's ass was rock solid too, and very nice, especially in those shorts she had on.

"Caitlyn." She said, turning around with a sweating glass of amber liquid in hand. Felicia took the glass, nodded, and took a sip.

The cool beer tasted great, and she could already feel herself relaxing, loosening up.

"How is it?" Caitlyn asked.

"Nice." Felicia said and took another sip.

"Good."

Felicia finished her sip and set the glass down.

"Did Janet say where she was heading?"

" I think she just had some errands to run, you know?"

Felicia nodded and took another sip. It really was refreshing, she was

starting to feel much more relaxed.

"What is this?" She asked, holding up the glass.

"Oh, it a new brew." Caitlyn said.

"It has a kick." Felicia said with another sip. Already her head was starting to swim.

"I hear it does. I haven't tried it though."

Felicia sat the glass down and noticed that it was going slightly out of focus. How much alcohol was in this?

A faint sound in the distance. Felicia raised her head, listening.

"What is it?" Caitlyn asked.

"I... I thought I heard..." Felicia listened. It sounded like, a mew? It was strange, muffled sound.

She turned her head towards the door to see if the sound was coming from outside and the whole room tilted. Felicia squeezed her eyes shut, waiting for the room to steady. It occurred to her that she hadn't eaten since yesterday afternoon, and drinking on an empty stomach was probably why the beer was hitting her so hard.

Her eyes opened and the room steadied for a brief moment, then resumed it's swimming. She heard the sound again, a muffled sound, like... like...

A scream. A muffled scream. Like someone screaming into a cloth. She knew the sound well because she had heard those very sounds coming from her own mouth.

She turned back to face Caitlyn when the swinging kitchen doors behind the bartender burst open. Caitlyn spun around, and out of the corner of her eye Felicia saw Eva shoot up.

A bound woman came hopping out of the double doors that lead to the kitchen. Felicia had to squint to see it all in focus. It wasn't just any bound woman, it was Janet! Her shirt had been pulled down to her waist and tied at the back, pinning her arms to her sides. A thick, white towel was pulled between her lips, gagging her. Janet appeared to be pants less, wearing a pair of thong panties that would be extremely sexy in different circumstances.

"MmmmHuurrmmm!" Janet's lips pursed around the gag as she pleaded with Felicia. Felicia could see Caitlyn and Eva both lunging for Janet. No, she couldn't let this happen!

Felicia shot to her feet and darkness crept into the corners of her vision. She felt herself sway and watched as Janet's eyes widened.

"Urrrmmm!" Janet tried to push forward, but Caitlyn and Eva had both grabbed an arm.

Felicia took a step and felt her feet go out from under her. The darkness spread, most of the world going dark around her as she fell. Before everything went black, she caught sight of her beer and realized that they had probably slipped something in it.

Her vision went black and she felt herself hit the floor. The last thing she heard was Janet's muffled screams.

Then it all went silent.

23.

The warehouse was disgusting, even as far as bad guy hideouts went. Though Gina didn't consider herself an authority on the subject of abandoned warehouses, she did spend several days bound, gagged, and naked in one, so she did know a thing or two about it. A small part of her pitied Felicia for having to be stashed here, but only a small part.

It's more than she ever deserves. Gina thought and sat back in the office chair, one of the only pieces of non-rotted furniture in the building. Her and her girls had arrived in the town of Marston's Pointe a few days back and had no trouble finding a motel room. Marston's Pointe was a summer beach town, so a group of attractive women looking for a place to stay drew no attention. Very quickly though, Gina realized that if they were going to go through with their plan of kidnapping the Sheriff, a motel room would be a very hard place to stash her. Caitlyn and Eva spent a day searching before they found an old, broken down warehouse along a deserted stretch of beach. And now here Gina was, waiting.

The warehouse was small, with several rusted metal desks littered through out and their chairs. The ceiling had collapsed in several spots, letting in lots of sun and the sound of the waves outside. Bits of chipped paint and other debris covered the floors, as well as discarded food wrappers and beer cans. It was pretty evident that local kids used this place as a party destination, which was good, it meant the Sheriff wouldn't be alone here for long.

Gina crossed her long, toned legs and leaned back against the desk that stood next to her chair. She had dreamed of this day for what seemed like an eternity, dreamed of what she would do if she had Felicia bound and helpless in front of her, and now that day was finally here. The thought of the look on Felicia's face when she finally saw Gina made her smile.

Despite the decay around her, Gina tried to dress as best as she could for the situation. She guessed it was the same reason why you tried to look sexy when you knew you would be bumping into an ex: you wanted to rub it in their faces, you want them to see what they're missing. She wore a yellow, strapless halter top that perfectly showed off her round, exquisite breasts, dark blue daisy duke shorts to show off her legs and ass, and pumps. Part of her considered wearing the bikini that she had been kidnapped in, but she could never bring herself to wear it that one again. Once she had gotten free, she swore that she would never be a victim again, and that bikini was a daily reminder of that, and of Felicia's betrayal. The thought of it all still stung, after all this time, knowing that Felicia was behind it all.

Gina loved Felicia like a sister, had brought her under her wing, but she didn't count on Felicia inspiring her as much as she did. Felicia's passion for law enforcement, her spirit, the fight in her, Gina had never met a woman more driven, and it caused her to question everything about herself. She once thought that she was content to live her life as she had been: modeling, working out, doing pageants, designing bikinis, etc, but then she saw how Felicia wanted to make a difference, to help people. After much thought, Gina had decided to enroll in Criminal Justice school, and thought Felicia would be ecstatic, that they could make a difference together, but Felicia reaction turned out to be much different.

The modeling world was a tough business, full of backstabbers and people out for themselves, and it hurt Gina to find that Felicia would sink so low, that Felicia was just like the others, if not worse.

And now here was Felicia wearing a Sheriff's badge and making a mockery of it. Gina saw the newspaper with the photo of Felicia bound and gagged in her underwear and probably stared and laughed at it for far too long. Poor Felicia wasn't even aware that was the beginning of her troubles.

At the far end of the warehouse, a door opened and sunlight filtered in. Female voices brought Gina back to the moment and she sat up, waiting. After all this time, now she would finally have her moment. She could see Caitlyn and Eva heading towards her, a bound female form held struggling between them. Gina smiled.

Her smiled faded when she saw that the woman held between them wasn't Felicia at all. Fuck! She gave them a photo and everything, how could they botch this. This woman, though beautiful, didn't look even close to Felicia. The woman was older, with brown, highlighted hair and dark rimmed glasses. A thick, white towel gagged her, and the woman's shirt was pulled down around her waist and knotted in the back, pinning her arms down to her sides and exposing her large breast that were barely contained by her bra. Her pants were down around her ankles and also tied, and the woman wore a pair of skimpy thong underwear. Gina recognized Eva's work when she saw it, that Latina spent far too much time thinking of ways to tie people up, frankly it disturbed Gina.

The woman, the prisoner, widened her eyes at the sight of Gina and mumbled something incoherent into her gag.

"Glllubb! Mmmlllellppp! Ullllumm!" She said, her breasts bouncing as she pulled against Eva and Caitlyn.

Gina stood, sighed, and shook her head.

"This... this isn't her. Come on guys! Now what are we going to do?"

"We know Gina, this is her buddy." said Caitlyn with a smile on her face.

This didn't make Gina any happier, what the hell were they supposed to do with this chick? Gina didn't want to drag anyone else into this mess than she had to.

"Yeah but... ughhh..." She sighed and pointed towards the corner. "Just tie her over their until I can figure out what to do with her." Gina rubbed her eyes as she spoke.

Caitlyn dragged the struggling woman over to the pillar while Eva grabbed some rope from on top of the desk. A rusty beam jutted down from a hole in the roof, rust and corrosion having eaten a hole through the metal of the beam itself. Eva threw a length of rope through the hole in the beam while Caitlyn held onto the prisoner. The rope fed through the hole and Eva tugged on it to see if it would hold. Gina held her breath, if that beam didn't hold the whole roof would come down on them.

It held, and Eva motioned for Caitlyn to bring the prisoner over. She did, and held the woman's arms while Eva ripped the shirt away from the woman's waist. Then they raised the woman's arms above her head and tightly tied them with the rope hanging from the beam. Once Eva was satisfied that the woman's hands were secured above her head, she squatted down and pulled the pants away from her ankles. The woman tried to kick at her captor but Caitlyn held her feet and soon Eva had her feet bound together with a length of rope.

The Latina stood and smiled at her bound prisoner, then gripped either side of her thong panties.

"HRRRUMMPH!" The woman's went wide and she tried to pull back and Eva prepared to pull down her panties.

"Wait, wait!" Gina shouted, moving towards them. Eva let go of the woman's panties and spun to face Gina.

"What are you doing?" Gina asked.

"I just... its-"

"Leave her, Jesus. Look, why did you kidnap her and not Felicia?"

"Oh we have Felicia too?" Caitlyn said.

Gina's jaw dropped.

"What?" She asked.

"We have Felicia too, she's out in the car."

Gina balled her fists.

"Why aren't you getting her?"

"Well, they've been feisty, and it would be pain to drag them both in at the same time, and we weren't sure what you wanted to do with this one, and we had to gift wrap Felicia, and-

"Enough, enough," Gina cut Caitlyn off. "Just go, bring her in here, okay?"

"Okay." Caitlyn nodded and motioned to Eva. Eva gave the bound woman a look of disappointment and followed her partner out of the warehouse.

That left Gina alone with this woman, Felicia's friend. Gina locked eyes with the bound, half naked woman.

"I'm really sorry about this, I don't know how you got mixed up in all this."

"Hrrrummmph!" The woman rolled her eyes.

"If I let you go, can you promise to keep your mouth shut?" Gina asked, hopeful.

"Ummmm mmmmhhhmm!" The woman shook her head, eyes blazing.

Gina sighed and hung her head.

"Look, if you knew Felicia like I knew her, then you wouldn't be so lucky. She would leave you tied here in order to save her own skin."

"Grrrr" The woman glared at her.

"Have it your way then." Gina turned away just in time to Caitlyn and Eva dragging another bound form into the warehouse. She took her seat, crossed her legs, and smiled, ready for her moment, to face Felicia again.

But her smile faded and turned into a look of confusion. The figure that Eva and Caitlyn carried between them was cocooned from head to toe in metallic red wrapping paper. The only sign that it was a person was from the struggling and muffled protests. From within.

"Ummmm! Mmmmm! Glllmmm!" The figure wriggled in the two women's hands. The wrapping paper really did wrap Felicia, if it was Felicia, from top to bottom. Red ribbon held the paper in place and formed a large bow at her front. Gina's jaw dropped, she thought that when they said gift wrapped they meant...whatever.

Gina, jaw still agape, got to her feet. Caitlyn and Eva came to a stop a few feet in front of her, a satisfied smile on both of their faces. Between them, the wrapped woman continued to struggle.

"Ullllummmmph! Mmmmmmph!"

"Wha-What is this?" Gina asked. The smiles faded.

"Her idea." Caitlyn said and nodded to Eva, who kept smiling.

"Aren't you going to open your present?" Eva asked, motioning to the bound woman.

"Mlllllgrrrmmmph!"

Gina rubbed her eyes once again.

"Just... get her out of that." She sighed.

Eva sighed and grabbed the bow and ribbon wrapped around her prisoner and pulled while Caitlyn grabbed the red wrapping and tore at it from the back. At first the wrapping fell free from around Felicia's head. She shook her brown hair free and huffed into her gag as the girls worked away at the rest of the wrapping around her.

"Hummmph! Mmmmph!" Felicia's attention was on Caitlyn and Eva as they pulled the wrapping paper from her body.

The last of the wrapping paper was pulled away and Felicia wobbled on her bound feet. Both Caitlyn and Eva took one of her bound arms to steady her and she turned forward to follow their gaze. Her eyes widened like saucers upon seeing Gina.

Gina's eyes also widened. She was expecting to see Felicia bound, in fact had given express directions to have her bound and gagged, but... Eva had gone to town in an extreme way. Felicia was completely naked, and what looked like red, velvet ribbon was wrapped around her mouth, and Gina assumed that the other side of the ribbon was adhesive of some sort so that it kept Felicia's lips sealed shut. Her hands were bound behind her, presumably with the same ribbon, and the ribbon was wrapped around her ankles and above her knees. It was also wrapped around her chest, covering Felicia's nipples and pushing her breasts up and in. Her chest heaved and her bare breasts pushed against the binding ribbon as she stared at Gina.

The ribbon was also wrapped around Felicia's waist and held a large, red bow in place over her bare crotch. It also looked like ribbon ran

down from the bow between Felicia's legs and up through her ass
cheeks.

Gina was too distracted by the absurdity in front of her to notice
Felicia staring, wide eyed like she had seen a ghost. After a moment,
Felicia snapped back to reality and tried to pull away from her
captors.

"Urrrummmph!" She turned her head and tried to pull away but
Caitlyn and Eva held her tight.

Gina too, was brought back to reality and allowed a smile to spread
across her face. Eva grabbed Felicia by the cheeks and turned her
head to face Gina.

"Glllummph!" Felicia protested.

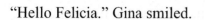

"Hello Felicia." Gina smiled.

"Grrrrmmmmmmph!" Felicia flexed, straining against the ribbon that held her. Her nude body twisted and writhed, showing off her exquisite muscles as she tried to pull away.

"Set her down girls, let's talk." Gina moved towards her desk chair and took a seat.

Eva held onto Felicia while Caitlyn stepped away and grabbed an old, crumbling desk chair and rolled it over. Felicia never stopped struggling.

"Hrrrummph! Mmmmmpph! Glllummph!"

Gina watched and smiled. Caitlyn set the chair a few feet in front of Gina and Eva deposited her prisoner in in it.

"Ullllummmgullpph! Mmrrrrrgggllle!" Felicia twisted in the chair.

"Felicia." Gina said calmly.

The girl didn't stop struggling, and started to kick her bound feet.

"Felicia."

"Mrrrrrmmpph!"

"Felicia!" Gina shouted. Felicia stopped and stared, her brown hair hanging in a tangle around her red gag.

"Long time no see? I see that you've been busy. How's being sheriff treating you?"

"Grrrrmmmm..." Felicia narrowed her eyes at Gina.

"Did you get the bikini I left for you? It's my newest design, I thought it would look good on you."

Upon hearing this, Felicia let out a squeak and sat back, her eyes quizzical. So she did find the bikini.

"I saw your newspaper article, looks like you've been having a rough time of things. I thought I would stop by and visit. It's been so long.

Felicia now sat in rapt attention, watching, listening.

"This is quite the reversal isn't it? Last time you saw me, I was the one naked, bound and helpless. Do you remember that?"

"Ummm mmmm!" Felicia shook her head.

"Oh you must, those men came in a snatched, carried me off to a dark, dingy place not too different from where we are now."

"Muummph! Nmmmmphh!" Felicia shook her head.

"I spent three days, tied up and gagged with those men, while they waited. Apparently they had been hired to kidnap me, but their benefactor never paid up. They waited, and waited, apparently they were going to receive further instructions along with the rest of the money. I had to listen, unable to talk or to reason with them, as they debated what to do with me. If they should just leave me, or let me go, or put me in a box, fill it with cement, and dump me in the ocean. Can you imagine what that's like?"

"Ulllummmp Mmmm!" Felicia nodded.

"I guess you can, looks like something similar happened to you not that long ago. In the end, the men never received their payment, and decided to leave. They were sure that someone would be looking for a "hot chick" like me and I would be found in no time. I wasn't, though I waited, and waited. No one came. No one was looking for me, Felicia."

Felicia was still now, waiting, watching.

"I found a rusty piece of metal and used that to cut myself free, but I was still naked and alone with no idea of where I was. Then I noticed that one of the men must have dropped their phone when leaving." Gina continued while Felicia sat on edge.

"It must have been a burner phone, because it was deactivated, but it did have the emails sent from whoever hired them. So I held onto it and left the warehouse where they had me. It wasn't that different from here, abandoned, set on a beach. Can you imagine what it's like having to sneak naked along a beach? Too embarrassed to ask anyone for help?"

Felicia still didn't move, just listened.

"But I made it home, everyone was wondering where I was, everyone asked if I was okay, except you." Gina looked right into Felicia's eyes. Felicia had gone pale, like her blood had turned to ice.

"Hrruuummph?" She asked.

"I didn't see you at the gym, I found you had stopped competing because you were getting more modeling jobs. Apparently my agency had dumped me because I skipped few shoots because I was tied up. No other bikini pageants would take me because I no showed at one. But I still had friends, including a few guys with IT skills."

Felicia started shaking and avoided Gina's gaze.

"They traced the email address of whoever hired those men to your IP address. I suddenly realized why you never bothered to check on me, to call the police. You hired them."

Felicia lifted her head and looked Gina in the eye. Looking over Felicia's shoulder, Gina could see that her friend, still bound and gagged, was staring at Felicia wide eyed.

"Mrrrggle! Ulllummph! Mmmlllllppph! Urrrmmph! Shmmmph!" Felicia protested.

"Trying to explain yourself? Beg forgiveness?"

"Ummmph! Mmmmmmph!" Felicia nodded.

"Too late. And now I see that you're a Sheriff of your own cute little beach town, how's that going for you?"

"Ulllummmph!" Felicia protested.

"From where I sit, it doesn't look like you've done a great job. In fact, you're a public embarrassment, not only to the police department, but this town. The cute former model that thought she could be a Sheriff and gets tied up in her underwear on the first day."

"Grrrrr" Felicia grumbled.

"I think this town needs a new face, someone who can really clean it up," Gina reached into her pocket and pulled out a shiny, gold, sheriff's badge. "Someone like me," she smiled.

Felicia's eyes went wide.

"Ulllummmmph! Mmmmph! Mmmmmph!" her head shook furiously.

"And I even have two deputies I can trust," Gina motioned to Caitlyn and Eva standing a few feet away. "Because Sheriff Fetters decided to leave town amid public pressure due to her disgrace, but not before appointing a successor."

"Ullllummph! Mmmmph!"

"As for you, I'll leave you as you left me, alone and forgotten. Silent except for your thoughts."

"MMMMRRRRRMMMPH!" Felicia shook her head, eyes blazing.

Gina motioned to the other woman, Felicia's friend.

"I am sorry about her, I really am, but I didn't want anyone else to get mixed up in this. But now she knows what kind of a woman you really are."

Felicia twisted around and met the other bound woman's gaze. The woman lowered her eyes and shook her head.

"Ullllm?" Felicia questioned.

"Someone will find you, looks like this place is a popular party spot, or you'll get free. Whatever happens, don't come back for me Felicia. Leave town, go back to L.A. Forget about me and this place." Gina stood and Felicia twisted her head up at her, glaring.

"Grrrrmmmmm!" Her eyes narrowed into slits and her face reddened.

"This is my town, and I'm going to succeed where you would have failed. I'm going to clean it up, because I take whatever you do and do it better."

At this Felicia shot up, her eyes turning to fire.

"GRRRMMMPH! MMMMLLLUMMMMPH! UMMMPPH!"
Felicia hopped forward to tackle Gina, but Gina took a step back and Felicia plunged forward, crashing onto the dirty, hard floor of the warehouse.

Gina looked down at her bound captive, at the ribbon cleaving Felicia's chiseled ass cheeks. Felicia's cheeks were clenching as the woman wriggled around on the ground, grumbling into her gag as she did. It was such an absurd sight that Gina couldn't help but giggle a bit.

Felicia rolled over onto her back and glared at Gina.

"Grrrmmmmm!" Was her reply.

"Bye Felicia!" Gina blew her a kiss and headed towards the door, motioning for Caitlyn and Eva to follow.

"Mrrrmmmm! Ullllummmm!" Felicia moaned into her gag.

Caitlyn and Eva stepped out of the warehouse and Gina gripped the door handle to follow.

"Urrrmmmmm! Mmmmmm-"

Gina slammed the door behind her, cutting off Felicia's muffled cries.

24.

"Mmmmrrrrrghhh! Ulllmmm! Grrrrmmmmble!" Felicia moaned into her gag as she wriggled helplessly on the floor. Still bound and gagged, Janet had no choice but to watch helplessly as this woman she had shared her bed with was reduced to a helpless, moaning damsel. For what seemed like the thousandth time, Janet tugged on the bonds that kept her hands suspended above her but they held firm. Whoever these people were, they knew their knots.

"Ummmph!" Felicia was on her knees now, hanging her head in defeat. Janet couldn't take her eyes off of the now helpless Sheriff. It was one thing to be bound and gagged, but Felicia was completely nude and wrapped up in a bow like a sadistic present. Beneath the bonds, Felicia's lithe muscles flexed as she once again strained against the ribbon that constricted her.

"Grrrrmmmmm.... urrrmmmm" Her nude body tensed as she tried to use all of her strength to break her bonds, but it was no use, the ribbon held tight.

"Urrrmmmm" Felicia sat back, hanging her head once again, and went silent.

Janet watched and waited. They couldn't give up now! That woman, Gina, couldn't just leave them, could she? But she had said Felicia did the same to her. She replayed the things Gina had said over in her mind, that Felicia had paid someone to kidnap her, and then left Gina bound and naked, could it be true? That didn't sound like Felicia.

But she watched Felicia's eyes as Gina talked and knew it to be true, knew that Felicia wanted to explain herself but couldn't because of the gag. Felicia had ruined this woman's life and Janet got caught in the crossfire, and Gina seemed almost sad about it all. Sad that Janet had gotten caught up in it, sad that Felicia had betrayed her like that. And now here they were, trapped and waiting.

Felicia still had her head down and was sitting on the filthy floor, all she had now was her thoughts to keep her company. Janet realized that she couldn't let this happen, couldn't let Felicia retreat into her head, couldn't leave them here waiting for someone to stumble on them.

"Mmmm!" Janet mumbled into her gag.

Felicia didn't raise her head.

"Grrrrmmm! Ummmm!" Janet called out. It was hard to give a pep talk when you're chewing on a cloth.

But still, Felicia didn't look up.

"GRRRRMMMMMPPH!" Janet squealed, eyes blazing.

Finally Felicia raised her head and met Janet's eyes. Felicia's eyes were heavy, filled with regret, and guilt.

"Urrrmmm mmrrrgggglll!" Janet never took her eyes off of Felicia and tugged on her hands.

"Urrrmm?" Felicia shrugged.

"Mrrrrmmmph!" Janet tugged on her bonds again, hoping Felicia would get the hint.

"Urrrmmmm..." Felicia leaned her head back, clearly not getting the hint.

"Mmmmrrrrummm-" Janet started to let loose a tirade into her gag when the beam above her shifted forward, raining a light dusting of drywall and dirt down on her head.

Janet froze. Felicia lifted her head and stared wide eyed.

"Ummmmm" Janet mewed into her gag, and the beam shifted forward again. Apparently it was not as stable as their captors thought.

"Urrrrmmmmpph!" Felicia started using her legs and feet to pull herself forward, steadying herself with her hands bound behind her.

"Urrrmmm!" Janet moaned as the beam shuddered again. If it came down, it would come down right on her head!

Felicia leaned her weight forward and pushed herself up with her powerful legs. She wobbled as she tried to steady herself.

"Urrrmmmblle!" Janet muttered words of caution to Felicia as she tried to stand. The muscles in Felicia's legs bulged as she pushed herself into a standing position-

-And held it. Felicia stood, balancing on her bound feet, and hopped towards Janet.

The beam shuttered forward.

Felicia hopped a few feet forward, her breasts bouncing and heaving as she moved closer to Janet.

"Mrrrmmmph!" Janet called to Felicia. If this beam came down, she didn't want it coming down on both of them.

Another hop and Felicia grew closer. The beam creaked and lowered, showering more plaster onto Janet.

"Mmmmmph!" Janet cried.

And Felicia was there, a few feet away from Janet. The naked Sheriff steadied herself and narrowed her eyes at Janet.

"Ummm mmm! Ummm mmmm!" Janet shook her head, knowing what Felicia had planned.

The beam was hanging precariously now, hovering just above Janet's head. Felicia's legs tightened and she pitched herself forward. Her bound body collided into Janet's.

The beam came loose and cut forward. Janet and Felicia tumbled back-

-But Janet's hands were still bound to the beam and she was carried forward, following the path of the heavy steel. Her momentum carried her into Felicia and they both went down.

The beam landed nose first into the ground and tilted forward, away from the bound women. It landed with a loud crash. Felicia and Janet pressed their bodies against each other as chunks of ceiling crashed around them.

And then everything went silent. Janet opened her eyes and found herself looking into Felicia's. Her eyes were wide, terrified.

"Urrmmm mmmmpph!' Janet let out a sight of relief.

"Urrmmm glllllmmph!" Felicia let out what almost could have been a laugh.

Suddenly Janet was aware of how close they were. She could feel Felicia's bare breasts pressing against hers, the steady rise and fall of her chest, Felicia's legs rubbing against hers. Without thinking, Janet leaned forward and nuzzled her gagged mouth against Felicia's. Felicia returned the gesture.

Janet leaned forward and realized that she could move her hands, the beam falling must have broken the rope around it. She brought her hands up and wrapped them around Felicia's back. Felicia leaned forward and rubbed her crotch against Janet's and Janet could feel the heat from her body, the ribbon over her crotch moistening.

Janet's hands drifted down to Felicia's bare buttocks and dug into her soft skin. In that moment, Janet didn't care what Felicia had done to that Gina woman, or that they were still bound. All that mattered was that they were alive and in each other's arms. She rolled Felicia onto her back and rolled on top of her. One of her hands stroked Felicia's bare breasts while the other ripped her own gag off. She had enough of being silenced.

"Mrrrmmmppph..." Felicia closed her eyes and moaned in pleasure.

Janet's hungry hands found the ribbon around Felicia's breasts and ripped it away, exposing the Sheriff's nipples. She leaned forward and flicked her tongue along Felicia's bare breasts while her hand drifted down towards the woman's crotch.

"Urrrrmmppphh...." Another moan into her gag. Janet's hand found the ribbon over Felicia's crotch and ripped it away.

"Mmmmmm!" Felicia moaned and gyrated.

Janet's finger traced Felicia's left breast, down her body, over her stomach, and finally her crotch. She traced it along Felicia's thigh and the Sheriff shuddered and moaned again.

Then Janet's finger ran along Felicia's moist lips and her bound feet kicked in pleasure. Her finger danced the outer edges of Felicia's vagina and then found it's way inside her.

"Ummmmph!" Felicia contorted and Janet hooked her finger up and inside the bound woman.

Another moan of pleasure. Janet continued to work her finger inside Felicia.

Felicia moaned and twisted her lithe body as Janet worked her inside.

"MMMMMMMPHH!" Felicia exclaimed and Janet felt her come.

25.

Janet and Felicia quickly ripped away the rest of their bonds and stood amidst the ruins of the warehouse, suddenly aware of their nudity. As soon as they got free, they set about trying to find some thing to cover up.

And had no luck. Both woman hoped to find at least an old towel or cloth to cover up, but there was nothing but dirt and dust in the warehouse. Janet was less worried about preserving her modesty since she had spent considerable time on the beach in bikinis just as revealing as the underwear she was wearing, but poor Felicia was completely nude. Felicia was becoming more and more self conscious and placed one hand over her breasts and another over her crotch.

"What now?" Janet asked, knowing that they had to get out of the warehouse somehow.

"We have to get to the Sheriff's station, stop Gina." Felicia said.

"Yeah but..." Janet motioned to Felicia's lack of clothes and the fact that she was in lingerie.

"This is on the beach right?" Felicia asked.

Janet nodded.

"I live along the beach, we'll have to sneak along to my place."

"Do you really think we can get by unnoticed?" Janet asked.

"We'll have to," Felicia shrugged. "We can't let her win."

She turned and strode towards the doorway, baring her naked ass towards Janet.

"Felicia wait." Janet called.

Felicia stopped and turned.

"What Gina said back there. I need to know if it's true." Janet said.

Felicia grew solemn and hung her head.

"I was stupid and made a very bad decision. It went very, very wrong and I couldn't face myself or Gina after it. I've spent every day since wishing I could take it back."

Janet nodded.

"Fine, after this is over, and we're wearing more clothes, we'll talk more."

Felicia nodded and headed towards the door.

26.

"Ian, it's not going to oil up itself!" Tanya called again to her son, who was doing his best to ignore her.

Ian sat on a beach chair, wearing a black t-shirt, she swore that was all he owned, gray shorts, and large headphones covering his ears. He stared at his cell phone like a man hypnotized. They were both sitting by her pool, though neither of them seemed interested in actually getting in the water.

"Ian!" She held up a bottle of tanning oil in his general direction and shook it. Tanya was stretched out on her stomach in a beach chair, wearing what she told everyone was her favorite bikini, her white thong bikini, when in fact it was her only bikini, and she looked great in it.

Her son ignored her though and continued to stare at his phone. He was getting to be so difficult these past few months. She told herself it was because he was 16 and that was to be expected, but this... When he wasn't ignoring her, he was arguing with her, telling her to stop wearing the bikini, to spend less time by the pool, not to chase any more crime stories. It almost made her like when he ignored her.

Tanya sighed and got off the chair. She didn't want her ass cheeks to burn, but couldn't reach behind to oil them up herself. It was time Ian learned to respect his mother. In a few strides she was across the pool deck and ripped the headphones from his ears.

"Hey!" He shouted, grasping for them as she pulled them towards her.

"No, not until..." She held out the bottle of tanning oil. Ian back away, repulsed.

"I'm not rubbing my hands all over your ass." He said. Tanya turned around, baring her full cheeks to him.

"Yes you will! I'm not burning!" She huffed. Ian was doing his best not to stare and instead focused on the still waters of the pool.

"Then stop wearing that stupid thing. You're too old for it anyway."
He got up and started to head towards the house.

"Uh!" She huffed and wheeled around to face him. "Well you know what, that's it for these expensive ass headphones of yours!" She shouted and raised her hand, intending to toss his headphones into the pool.

Ian cried out and grasped at her hand but stopped.

"Ah hah! Now are you going to listen to your mother?" She asked, but then noticed that he wasn't even looking at her. His eyes were focused on something on the beach behind her.

"Ian?" He didn't respond and just stared off into space. "Ian!" She snapped her fingers but it didn't break his concentration. Tanya sighed and figured that she may as well see what is so fascinating and spun around to face the beach. What she saw made her jaw drop.

Sheriff Fetters and what looked to be Janet Rossi were hurrying up the beach as fast as they could go. Janet Rossi was wearing what looked like a bra and a skimpy pair of thong panties, and Sheriff Fetters was completely nude, one hand placed over her bare breasts and another over her crotch. Tanya realized that she never fully got to see what kind of body the Sheriff had, and for a moment she was just as mesmerized as her son. Fetters was amazing, tight and tone, and completely tan. And her ass, my God, her ass was tight, completely solid, a work of art. Even Janet Rossi kept herself in great shape, and Tanya realized that she didn't know how great Janet's breasts were until this moment, seeing them bounce up and down, barely contained by her somewhat small bra.

Wait, what the hell were they doing on the beach like that? Were they an item? She decided this warranted some investigating, but first-

She spun around and placed a hand over her son's eyes. Ian cried out and pulled away.

"Hey! Mom!" he protested, shoving her hand down.

"No! Go inside!" She ordered.

"What... no!" He stammered, searching for a suitable excuse to stay outside.

"Inside! It's rude to stare!" She motioned to the door. Ian glared at her and snuck another look over her shoulder.

"Hey!" She said and once again pointed to the back door. Ian hung his head and turned around. Tanya turned to the beach to see Sheriff Fetters and Janet entering the Sheriff's yard through her back gate. Both women froze when they saw Tanya watching.

"Hey, what do you think you're doing! There are children around!" She screamed.

"Mom I'm not a kid!" Ian protested.

"Inside!" She shouted. Meanwhile, Janet and the Sheriff were heading towards the back door to the house.

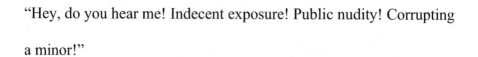

"Hey, do you hear me! Indecent exposure! Public nudity! Corrupting a minor!"

Felicia stopped and glared at Tanya, taking her hand away from her breasts and crotch. Behind her, Tanya heard Ian gasp. The Sheriff placed her hands on her hips and stood defiant and nude on her back deck, staring down Tanya.

"Who are you going to call? I'm the Sheriff!" She spat at Tanya.

Tanya stammered, looking for words.

"You know what Tanya? Kiss my ass!" Sheriff Fetters spun around, stuck her perfect rear out, and smacked either cheek. Ian gasped again and Tanya worried that he would have a heart attack.

Then Sheriff Fetters strode across her deck, opened her back door, ushered Janet inside, and closed it behind them.

27.

It occurred to Felicia that it was fitting that earlier she found herself borrowing Janet's clothes and now here had to return the favor. In the end, Janet took a pair of black workout pants which were a little too tight in the rear, though a small part of Felicia didn't mind this, they made Janet's ass look amazing. Janet also borrowed a t-shirt which was also a little too small, accentuating Janet's already large breasts. As for Felicia, she slipped on a pair of black thong panties and a matching black bra, then threw on one of her spare Sheriff's shirts. As she buttoned up her shirt, she realized this was her last one, somehow she had made a strange habit of losing her clothes in the line of duty.

She also made a habit of getting tied up in the line of duty, but not anymore. Felicia stared at her reflection in the full length mirror in her bedroom. Her shirt was buttoned up only halfway, exposing her black bra and cleavage underneath. Turning around, Felicia saw that the shirt was long enough to cover half of her ass. Here she was, the model turned Sheriff, fighting now not only to save her town, but her reputation and job. In that moment, she realized she had to be either the model or the Sheriff, but couldn't be both.

Turning back around, she finished buttoning up her shirt, leaving on button open just beneath her neck. Then she headed over to her closet and pulled out a pair of black cargo pants, standard police issue. If she wanted to be a cop, she had to dress like a cop. She slipped the pants on, tucking her shirt in, then secured them with a belt. Once again she looked at herself in the mirror, with the baggy pants and tucked in, buttoned up shirt, she looked like a cop. Lastly, she tied her hair back into a ponytail. Hell would freeze over before she let Gina and her cronies run her town, not while there was work to be done.

Fully dressed and ready for action, Felicia found Janet waiting in the kitchen. Janet eyed her up and nodded approvingly.

"You look ready for action." She said.

Felicia nodded in thanks.

"Gina and her girls will most likely be at the station, with the rest of the force there I can easily cuff them and lock them up. I can drop you at the bar on the way there."

Janet shook her head.

"Are you kidding? These women tied us up and left us half naked-or in your case, naked-in a dingy warehouse? I want to be there to see you take care of them."

Felicia smiled and nodded.

"Fine, then maybe later I can use my handcuffs on you?"

Janet smiled back.

"Not a chance, you'll be the one being handcuffed."

"We'll see about that." Felicia smiled and turned towards the door. She imagined that once this was all said and done, she wouldn't feel a bit bad about seeing Gina restrained again.

28.

The drive to the station seemed like ages. Felicia tried to play every scenario over and over in her head, hoping to account for anything that could go wrong. She expected resistance from Gina, even from her fellow officers because she had to face it, they didn't seem to like her that much. It was probably a good thing that Janet chose to come along because Janet could serve as a witness and corroborate everything Felicia said. Kidnapping an officer of the law, and impersonating one, was a big charge and Gina and her cronies would spend a long time in jail for it.

Part of her still couldn't believe that Gina was back. Another part of her couldn't blame Gina for being angry, for wanting justice. Real justice would have been to call the police on Felicia though, not leave her bound and gagged in a warehouse. She thought back to that moment, being wrapped up like a Christmas present, trying to explain herself to Gina, trying to apologize, but unable because of the sticky ribbon keeping her mouth shut. Her frustration was red and blinding, burning deep into her soul, and she hoped that she could use that, channel it into strength and break free of her bonds. But the ribbon held tight and all she could do was strain against it and grow more and more frustrated. Maybe instead of arresting Gina, she should tie her and her buddies up, stick them in a box, and ship them out like Jack wanted to do with her.

But no, that would only continue the cycle. They would be arrested and tried, but another thought occurred to her: if they went to trial, it would no doubt get out that Felicia had Gina kidnapped. News like that would destroy her career in law enforcement, and there would be no way the modeling world would take her back after hearing that she pulled a stunt like that.

In that moment, she decided so be it. Maybe it was time for the news to get out, maybe it was time she had this weight lifted, at least it would all be over.

In the passenger seat, Janet sat on edge, tapping her fingers against the window. Most of all, Felicia resented Gina for dragging Janet into this. Hopefully, once this was all said and done, Janet could return to her life. Felicia only hoped Janet would let her be a part of that life. So far, her stint in the town of Marston's Peak's had not been a successful one, but one good thing did come out of that: Janet, and she would fight to protect Janet through all of this.

The car pulled up outside the station and Felicia killed the engine. Her and Janet shared a look and nodded at each other. It was time to end this and get back to something that at least resembles normality.

"Whatever happens, stay behind me." Felicia said.

"You're sexy when you act like a cop." Janet purred. Felicia smiled back at her and exited the car. Janet followed.

The police station loomed in front of them. As they approached, Felicia noticed that there were no squad cars parked outside. Was everyone out on patrol? They entered and Felicia noticed that Deputy Cringe wasn't at her usual post by the door. Something was wrong, very wrong.

Felicia froze and looked around the station, noticing her office door was open at the back. She could see someone leaning against her desk waiting, arms crossed.

Gina.

Felicia backed up.

"Janet, let's-"

"Ummmmph!" Felicia spun around to see Gina's Latina friend wrap one arm around Janet's waist and clamp her free hand over Janet's mouth. The Latina smiled at Felicia as she dragged Janet away.

"He-UMMMMPH!" Felicia felt a hand clamp over her mouth and looked down to see a muscular arm, Gina's bodybuilder friend, wrap an arm around her chest and drag her back.

"Ullllummmgggpph! Mlllllmmph!" Janet continued to fight and kick as the Latina carried her towards an open door at the rear of the station, the holding cells.

"MMMMLLLLLLRRRRMMPH!" Felicia tried to fight, to protest, but the bodybuilder dragged her towards her office, towards Gina.

"Ullllmmmph!" Janet protested as the Latina twisted her around and through the door leading to the holding cells.

"MMMMMOOOOO! UMMMMMMMMPH!" Felicia tried to fight, but the bodybuilder twisted her around, bringing her face to face with a smiling Gina.

"Felicia, long time no see." She chuckled.

"GRRRLLUUUMMPH!" Felicia spat into the hand silencing her.

Gina strode forward and gave a "tsk tsk" motion with her finger.

"We received a call from a concerned citizen, a woman named Tanya, telling us about how the Sheriff and a woman named Janet

420

Rossi were streaking around the beach outside her home. In front of her son too, who's a minor. Apparently it's unbecoming of Marston's Pointe law enforcement to behave in such a way."

"GRRRMMMPH!" Felicia protested. Tanya! Once she got out of this, Tanya would pay for everything she had done these past few days.

"I dispatched your men to her place to get a statement, and conveyed to her that you are no longer a member of the police force. She didn't seem disappointed."

"Ulllummph!" Felicia protested.

"And I sent that Cringe woman home, boy is she unpleasant. Something will have to be done about her. Mostly, I wanted to get you here, alone, to avoid a scene. You're all too predictable."

Felicia glared at Gina. Footsteps came from the other end of the station and Felicia twisted her head to see the Latina emerging from the holding cells. Did she lock Janet up in there?

The bodybuilder's hand came away from Felicia's mouth.

"You won't get away with this? Where's Janet? What did you do with her? Once my men get here I'll tell them everything! You're all going to jail!"

Gina smiled.

"We'll have to make sure you don't talk much then. Get those clothes off her."

"What? No!" Felicia tried to kick but the Latina caught her foot and pulled off her boot while the bodybuilder held her tight. Her boot came off despite her kicking, and the Latina went to work on her other boot.

"Gina, do you know how much trouble you'll be in for this? All of you will spend your lives in jail!"

"Felicia, I gave you a chance to walk away. I'm actually impressed that you got free so fast. You should have left though."

"You know that I couldn't!" She spat at Gina.

"You never were that smart." Gina said.

"Hey!" Felicia cried out as her other boot was pulled off. Then the Latina reached up and gripped Felicia's belt.

"No! No! NO!" Felicia cried as the Latina undid the clasp on her belt. She felt the pants loosen. Then the Latina undid the top button on her pants.

"Stop! Stop!"

Gina looked at the Latina, then at Felicia, who continued to struggle. Her smile vanished and another look came over her face, it looked almost like regret, sorrow. It was there for a minute then vanished, replaced again by the smile. The fake smile, the modeling smile. The smile Gina flashed every time a camera went off, the smile she gave when she was posing up on a stage in her new bikini.

"Come on, hurry it up Eva." Gina said.

Eva lowered the zipper on Felicia's pants, exposing the front of her black, thong panties. Then the Latina gripped the waist of her pants and yanked down. Felicia cried out and kicked as Eva pulled the pants free of her kicking legs.

"Stop! Stop! I swear I'll get you all!" Felicia knew she was all out of threats, that they had her.

Behind her, the bodybuilder twisted her arms behind her back. Still smiling, the Latina leaned forward and undid the top button of Felicia's shirt.

"Where's Janet? Did you hurt her?"

"The less you struggle, the less time this will take, and you'll be able to see Janet again." Gina said.

"What did you do to her?" Felicia asked as the Latina undid more buttons.

"She could have just walked away, you didn't have to drag her into this again." Gina said

"She's my witness, she's going to help put you all away." Felicia said, noticing that her shirt was almost entirely undone.

Gina shook her head.

"Sadly its true. I wish there was another way." Gina shook her head as she spoke.

Then the buttons were undone and the Latina pushed Felicia's shirt back with zest. From behind, the bodybuilder grabbed the shirt and pulled it down past her arms. The Latina wrapped a surprisingly strong hand around Felicia's arm, keeping her from running off.

Then the shirt was off, and Felicia stood there in the middle of the police station in her underwear. The bodybuilder gripped Felicia's other arm with her vice like grip and handed the shirt to Gina with the other.

Gina reached out and took the shirt, looking down at it and back up to Felicia. Felicia tried to pull away but Gina's hench-woman had a firm grip on her. Then Gina put one arm through one sleeve.

"No!" Felicia pulled again as the woman held her.

Gina put her other arm through the other sleeve and pulled the shirt around her. She still wore her shorts, and as she buttoned up the sheriff's shirt it made it seem like she wore nothing underneath.

She stopped buttoning just below her large breasts, then took the bottom of the shirt and tied it up just above her shorts. Felicia couldn't help but think that if the other officers had a problem with how she dressed, wait until they see Gina.

Then Gina reached into her back pocket and took out the shiny, gold Sheriff's badge. She raised it up and pinned it to her shirt just above her right breast.

"What do you think?" Gina smiled. "New Sheriff in town."

Felicia pulled again.

"I will stop you." She said.

Gina laughed and motioned to the door to the holding cells.

"Lets book her!" She ordered, and they started dragging Felicia towards the cells.

"No! No! Let me go! Gina!"

They pulled Felicia through the door. Large, iron barred cells lined either side of the long hallway. Felicia struggled and fought as they pulled her down the corridor.

Gina closed the door behind her. It was heavy steel, and gave off a loud clang as it shut. Then Felicia's arms were twisted behind her.

"We'll have you cool your heels in here with your friend until we can come up with a more... permanent solution."

"Ow!" Felicia cried out as she felt the cold steel of handcuffs slapped onto her wrist. The cuffs clicked into place and she felt cuffs slapped on her other wrist and secured. They were tight, but left enough slack to not cuff off circulation. Then they were moving again, dragging Felicia down the corridor again. Her eyes widened when she saw a pile of clothes lying in the center of the corridor. They were her clothes, the ones she let Janet wear.

"Janet! Janet are you alright? Jan-ULLLLLLMMMPH!" A cloth was thrown over her head and pulled back between her teeth. It was thick, filling most of her mouth.

"Ullllmmm! Gllllmmm!" She mumbled and tried to shake off her gag. It was tight tight at the back of her head.

"There, that should keep you quiet." Gina said.

"Mmmmmm!" Felicia protested.

And they were moving again, down the hallway. Felicia fought and resisted as best she could but they were stronger than her.

And then she saw her, Janet. Once again, Janet was in her underwear. Her hands were cuffed behind her back like Felicia's and she was gagged with a thick, white cloth like Felicia. She was locked in one of the cells at the end of the block.

"Ulllmmmph?" Felicia called to her.

"Mmmmmmph!" Janet pressed against the bars of her cell, her large breasts protruding out from between the bars.

The door to the cell next to Janet's was open and Felicia was shoved in by her captors. She stumbled in, caught herself, and spun around to see the door slammed shut. Gina smiled as she produced a key and slid it into the lock.

"Grrrrrr!" Felicia cried and rushed forward.

Gina finished locking the door and stepped back as Felicia slammed herself against the bars.

"Grrrmmmph! Urgggglle! Gllllubbb!" Felicia mumbled incoherent insults at Gina.

"Make yourselves comfortable in here, ladies. You'll both be here for a while."

"Mmmmmeeepp!" Both Janet and Felicia yelped into their gags.

"And don't worry about anyone else stumbling upon you, I'll be the only one with the key to the cells."

"Mmmmm!" Felicia protested.

Gina stepped forward and glared at Felicia.

"You tried to get rid of me once and almost did, but you made a fool of yourself in the process. Now, you try to save this town and once again, you become a laughing stock, and to make it worse, you drag this poor woman into it with you." Gina motioned to Janet.

"Murrrggle! Urrrggle! Mmmph!" Janet replied and threw herself against the bars of her cell.

"Sit here and think about that. Meanwhile, myself and my new deputies," Gina motioned to the two women on either side of her. "Will succeed where you failed, we'll save this town. I was always better than you at anything you tried."

"Murrrrrmmmph!" Felicia spat.

Gina winked at her.

"Enjoy yourselves ladies. We'll talk soon" With that, she turned and stalked away, followed by her now deputies.

"Urrrrmmmph! Mmmmmmph!" Felicia called after them, watching as they went.

They never turned around. At the end of the corridor, they left

through the large metal door and slammed it behind them.

Then Felicia and Janet were alone, again. Felicia knew the door to

the holding cells was sound proof, no one outside would hear her or

Janet's muffled cries.

"Urrrrgggggphh!" Felicia turned to face the cell next to her. Iron bars

separated the cells, and Janet was pressed against them, staring at

Felicia.

Felicia stalked forward and leaned her head against the bars,

touching Janet's between them. Janet brought her gagged mouth up

and Felicia leaned forward and nudged Janet with her own gagged

mouth. Maybe they pull down each other's gags!

"Mmmmph... ummmph!" Janet moaned as they rubbed their faces against each other.

"Mrrgglle... ullmmmph..." Felicia moaned, rubbing her gag against Janet's.

But it was no use, they were tied tight. Janet pulled away and stepped back from the bars. Felicia watched as Janet turned around, baring her thonged ass towards her, and pressed her bare cheeks against the bars. The iron rod of the bar ran right between Janet's magnificent ass cheeks.

Felicia turned around and pressed against the bars of the cell as well. Her cuffed hands found the skin of Janet's ass cheeks and she ran her palms along them. Despite their captivity, there was so much she wanted to do to Janet, to dig her nails in, to smack them, to-

No, she had to focus on getting out, on stopping Gina, on stopping Ace.

She felt Janet's cuffed hands caress her own cheeks. A sigh escaped Felicia's gagged lips. Janet's touch felt amazing.

"Ullllmmmm..." Felicia moaned, feeling her skin break out in goosebumps.

As Felicia felt up Janet, and vice versa, she thought. They had to get out somehow, then deal with Gina and her cronies. But she needed help, and wasn't sure if she could count on her own officers to do so.

Then she remembered that one of them worked for Ace. Upon having this realization, she dug her nails in Janet's ass.

"Ulllmmm..." Janet moaned, but not in pain or discomfort. Felicia loosened her grip, but continued to run her palm up and down Janet's back side.

Janet moved slightly to the side so that the bars no longer bisected her cheeks and Felicia ran her fingers along Janet's ass towards her crack. Her hands found the thin fabric of the thong running through Janet's ass and she traced the fabric up. She found the top of the panties and wrapped her hands around the waist band and pushed down. As Janet's panties lowered, Felicia allowed her palms to once again slid along the older woman's backside.

Then Janet spun around, Felicia's bound hands moved along her hips, then her crotch. Janet pressed against the bars and Felicia hands found Janet's moist vagina. Her fingers traced along Janet's outer lips.

"Ullllmmm" Janet moaned.

Felicia found Janet's clit and twirled her finger along it. Janet writhed in pleasure.

"Ulllmmph! Mmmlllllph!"

Yes, Gina didn't know that one of the officers was dirty. And the guns were still in evidence, Ace would be coming for them any day now. Felicia rubbed her finger along Janet's clit, moving slightly faster.

"Ummmph! Mmmmp!" Janet moaned.

Any efforts that Gina and her girls made at getting Ace would be stymied by his inside man, they would be just as much of a laughing stock as Felicia.

She moved faster, feeling Janet's crotch get even more moist.

"Urrrrmmph! Mmmmmmpph!"

All Felicia had to do was wait, wait for Gina to fail. She also knew that Gina couldn't keep her in the cells forever, she would have to move her and Janet sooner rather than later. All Felicia had to do was wait, look for an opportunity.

Her other finger slipped inside Janet, hooking up and in.

"Mmmmmuuummmpph!" Janet exclaimed into her gag as she came.

Felicia felt Janet spin around and hook her cuffed hands around Felicia's panties. She felt Janet's hands run along her ass as she slid Felicia's panties off.

Felicia spun around to face Janet. It was her turn now.

And would be again.

End of Volume 1!

Felicia, Gina, and the rest of the girls will return...

And now a special preview of DAMSELS

ANONYMOUS VOLUME 2!

Though the junk yard was only a five minute walk away, Gina found

herself wishing that she would have worn better shoes. She wore a pair of purple wedges to match her bikini, which she fully intended

to take off as soon as she got to the party. Wedges were

uncomfortable, but they made Gina's butt look great. Gina was proud

of her ass, not too big, not too small, but just right, though it was

nothing compared to Felicia's butt, or even Jessica's. Felicia's ass

was a work of art, and something that Gina was always jealous of, as

she was sure Felicia was jealous of Gina's breasts, and Gina felt that

if they were ever combined, they would be the perfect woman.

The junkyard was an eyesore on the land, a large patch of twisted

dead metal surrounded by a rusty old fence. Gina wondered why it

was located so close to the casino but then guessed that most likely

Ace owned it as well. As she approached, Gina could see that the

metal gate hanging open. Jessica must already be here. She didn't

know what to expect when she walked through the gate, and wished

that she would have brought her gun as well. A badge was all well

and good, but if something went wrong, a badge wouldn't keep

people in line like a gun would.

Gina passed through the gate, tightening her grip on her shoulder bag. Mountains of twisted metal and garbage surrounded her on either side, wide walkways weaved through the dead cars like a labyrinth. Should she call out? Since Jessica had told her to come alone, Gina imagined that Jessica must also be alone herself, right?

"Jess?" She said softly as she continued to walk through the metal graveyard.

Nothing.

"Jessica? It's Gina!" She said, a little louder this time.

Gina came around a mound of junk and saw a large silhouette in the distance. A large crane hovered in the air, its claws hanging open like a bird's talons ready to strike. Below it she could see a long, elevated track sitting several feet off the ground: A conveyor belt. The belt lead to a large, rectangular, metal monstrosity: The car crusher.

The crane would pick cars up from the ground and drop them on the conveyor belt, which then dropped the cars into a small chamber where the massive, metal jaws of the crusher would compress the cars into small, metal blocks. Something about the thought made Gina cringe, but she couldn't dwell on that right now. She shook her head and pressed on, hoping that Jessica hadn't been held up by something.

"Jess!"

Gina came around another mound of junk and found herself by a small, wooden office shack. Like the rest of the junkyard, it seemed deserted.

"Jessica!" Gina called out, starting to get impatient.

"Shh!" Gina jumped and spun around to find Jessica, still clad in her gold bikini, stepping out of the wooden shack.

"Jesus Jess, you scared the hell out of-"

"Did you come alone?" Jessica's eyes were wide, terrified. Gina narrowed her gaze at the bikini clad woman.

"What's this about Jess?"

"Did... You... Come... Alone?" Jess said through gritted teeth.

"Yes, now what-"

"Were you followed?"

"What?" Gina rolled her eyes. What had Jess gotten herself into?

"Were you-" Jess started.

"No, I wasn't followed." Gina blurted.

Jessica let out a breath and stepped out of the shack. Her blond hair had dried and fell lazily around her shoulders. Gina was sure that the sight of two women in a junkyard in small bikinis presented a surreal image.

"I'm sorry, I just, I can't be too careful."

"It's alright Jess," Gina reached out an arm and stroked the woman's shoulder. "What's wrong?"

Jess's eyes continued to scan the junkyard around them, as if she was expecting enemies to materialize out of thin air.

"As you know, a man named Joseph Kingston, or "The King" as he calls himself, he runs the casino, contacted me asking if I could be the special "Celebrity Judge" for the Ms. Marston's Pointe Bikini Contest."

"I know." Gina nodded.

"He gave me a special Lady Luck Casino company email, to keep up with promotions, updates on the contests, etc. I would spend a few days in town, give their business some free publicity, and then leave, it would be easy."

"Okay..." Gina narrowed her eyes, not knowing where this was going.

"Except, I received an email I shouldn't have. Looks like King may have accidentally CC'd me on it. It was from him to someone named Ace."

"Ace?" Gina's eyes went wide.

"You know who this is?"

"A crime lord, practically runs the town."

"Shit! Dammit!" Jessica ran her hands through her hair, eyes wide.

"Jess, calm down!"

"Fuck, I... I knew this was bad, but I didn't know it was this bad!"
She began to pace back and forth, her muscle bound ass cheeks
clenching out of nervousness.

"Jess, calm down! I can help you. Did you read this email?"

"Of course I read it!" She cried out.

"Do you still have it?"

"Fuck no! As soon as I finished I deleted it, hoping that would be it, that they would just... leave it be, you know?"

"They didn't?" Gina shouldn't have asked, of course they didn't.

Jessica shook her head.

"I went out last night and came back to find that my hotel room was broken into. I grabbed my things and stayed at a shitty motel down the street."

"Why didn't you call me right away?" Gina asked.

"I just... I thought it was over? Maybe they were satisfied seeing that I deleted it. But all today I've noticed men following me, watching me."

"What did the email say?"

"That's why I brought you here, Ace owns this place as well as the Casino."

Gina nodded, her guess was right.

"And this is where they get rid of the bodies!" Jessica screamed.

Gina nodded again. It all made sense now.

"I thought that maybe if I brought you here, you could... you know, find evidence or something..." Jessica stared off as she spoke.

"Jess, look at me," Gina motioned to the bikini she wore. "I'm in no condition to perform an investigation. Let's get you back to the station, we'll have people protect you, then I'll come here and look around with a few other co-"

"No! No station, no cops!" Jessica's voice was frenzied, panicked.

"What do you mean? We can help you!" Gina was getting close to losing her patience with Jessica. She knew that the woman was scared, but she needed to work with Gina if she wanted to get out alive.

"There was more in the email, something about weapons in the police station..."

"A botched bust a month ago, yes." Gina said.

"Yes, and they want them back. Someone on the police force works for them!" Jessica shouted.

Gina's blood ran cold. One of her cops was dirty? This wasn't good. She stepped back and nodded, taking this news in.

"This person is going to help them take back the guns."

"Okay, okay," Gina held up a hand. "There's a few deputies that I trust, I'll leave you with them, then we'll go from there. Did this email say who it is that works for Ace?"

"Yes, it's someone named-"

Jessica froze. Gina's eyes widened. They heard footsteps approaching from somewhere in the yard. Voices grew closer.

"It came from over here!" A male voice said.

Gina met Jessica's terrified eyes.

"Run." Gina said.

Jessica didn't have to be told twice. She took off deep into the junkyard, and Gina followed.

Jess ran down a tight path between two junk piles, and Gina followed. As she ran, she thanked herself for all that cardio that she had to push herself through every morning. The junk piles seemed to be closing in on them as they ran, and Gina tried to ignore it and focus on the path ahead.

Jessica's ass cheeks jiggled and heaved as she ran. Gina was only a step behind her.

"Where do we go?" Jess asked.

"Keep running, maybe there's a back entrance." Gina said between breaths.

Somewhere behind the junk piles, they heard footsteps and quickened their pace.

"Didn't you bring a gun?"

"No!" Gina shouted.

"What kind of cop doesn't carry a gun everywhere?" Jess screamed.

"The cop that thinks she's going to a pool party!"

They rounded a corner and suddenly Gina felt herself pulled back.

Shit! They have me!

Jessica skidded to a stop.

"Gina!" she screamed.

Gina tried to press forward and heard a tearing sound. Looking down, she realized that her sarong had snagged on a twisted length of metal. The back portion of the sarong had ripped down the middle, exposing the small, purple thong running between her cheeks.

"Come on!" Jess shouted.

The footsteps were louder, closer.

Gina gritted her teeth and heaved forward and felt the fabric rip free of her body.

"Let's go!" She sprinted forward and Jessica took off too. Gina felt the wind on her butt cheeks, now bare thanks to her losing her sarong. The situation seemed to get more absurd with each passing moment.

The path opened up and they found themselves in clearing. In front of them were two paths between the junk.

"Which way?" Jessica asked.

Gina's eyes raced around, trying to find a path to freedom.

Then she noticed a half crushed in car lying a few feet away.

"Over here!" She grabbed Jessica's arm and pulled her towards the car.

***

Jack lead his men through a tight path through the garbage, following the sound of woman's voice. Two of them, in fact.

Who did this bimbo rope into this?

King was a smart guy, good with numbers, good with the businesses, but he fucked up big time. He and Ace were emailing and somehow

King accidentally sent a message to this Jessica chick, some sort of big time bikini model. The word from Ace was swift: Get rid of her.

They followed her to the junkyard and Jack realized how bad this situation was, the junkyard was where they disposed off... problems. That meant this chick had indeed read the email. Was she playing detective now? No matter, if she was at the junkyard, then that meant they could easily get rid of her.

But Jack heard another woman's voice in the junkyard too, so that meant that this Jessica chick had told someone about what she read. Shit, how many others did she tell?

Jack certainly hoped that Ace made King pay for this fuck up. Then again, Jack couldn't say anything, seeing how he was on Ace's shit list for the weapons fiasco, and failing to get rid of that cute Sheriff not once but twice.

But Jack had a plan to get the weapons back, and the Sheriff... well

she just disappeared, along with Janet Rossi, another thorn in Ace's

side. Word is that the Sheriff resigned and skipped town with Janet.

And apparently there was a new, even hotter Sheriff. This new

Sheriff hadn't run afoul of Jack or Ace yet, but she soon would, and

Jack couldn't wait to meet her.

He couldn't wait to tie her up.

As he moved down the path, Jack stopped. A frilly, purple garment

hanging from a piece of metal. Jack stepped forward and ripped it

from outcropping it was snagged on. It was a thin, purple fabric

decorated with gold sequins. It was like a skirt or something, Jack

had seen women wearing something like it at a beach to cover up

their swimsuits. So they had went this way.

He nodded for his men to press forward.

After a bit, the small path opened up into a wide clearing. At the other end of the clearing was two paths leading off deeper into the junkyard. He had brought six guys with him, and they stood on either side of him.

"What now boss?" One asked.

Jack looked at either path, knowing that each passing moment meant that these ladies were closer to getting away.

"Why don't we split, half go one way, half go another..." Jack turned his head to look around the area and his jaw dropped.

"What boss?" The goon asked.

Jack continued to stare, trying to make sense of what he was seeing.

"Boss, you want us to split up?"

Jack pointed to what he was looking at and pressed a finger to his lips.

Sitting in a corner in front of a massive pile of junk was a half destroyed car. It's entire back half was crushed, while the front was relatively intact. Two women were crouched down behind the smashed back half, their backs were to Jack and his men, seeing how the only thing he could see were their asses.

One ass was a deep bronze and very solid, and a gold thong bikini bottom ran through it. The other ass was lighter, and a purple thong cleaved this woman's much smaller but no less shapely rear end. He could also make out their legs bunched up in front of them. It was almost a clever plan, hide out and wait for the bad guys to run deeper into the junkyard. Almost clever, if only they found a better place to hide.

Jack's men smiled at him.

"Yes, let's split up. Half goes one way, half another. Meet back in a few minutes." He said loudly, then reached inside his coat and pulled a gun.

His men did the same.

Gina wrapped her arms around her long legs and leaned back against the car, waiting. The goons, or whoever they were chasing them, had bought it. They were going to split up, half follow one path, the others follow the other path. While they did so, Gina and Jessica would crawl out from behind the car and run back to the entrance of the junkyard, get Gina's car from the casino, and head back to the police station.

Everything went quiet. Jessica met Gina's eyes and smiled.

"Think they bought it?" She asked.

"Nope, but almost!" a male voice exclaimed from behind them.

Jessica screamed and jumped up.

"Wait!" Gina jumped up, reaching after Jess.

When Gina got to her feet, she saw that the car was surrounded on all sides by various large men dressed in black. All of them had their guns trained on the women. Gina threw her hands up, Jess did the same.

The man in charge, a built man with spiked up hair in a suit and tie, stepped forward.

"Hello ladies, I'm Jack. If you'll please follow me."

To be continued in Damsels Anonymous

Volume 2!